DC SUPER HEROES

STORYBOOK ★ COLLECTION

THIS TREASURY BELONGS TO

DC SUPER HEROES
STORYBOOK ★ COLLECTION

SUPERMAN
created by Jerry Siegel and Joe Shuster

BATMAN
created by Bob Kane

WONDER WOMAN
created by William Moulton Marston

HARPER
An Imprint of HarperCollinsPublishers

★ TABLE OF CONTENTS ★

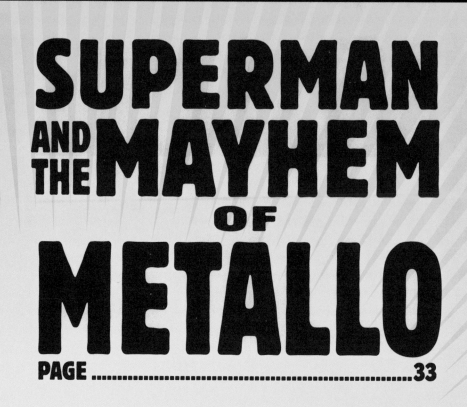

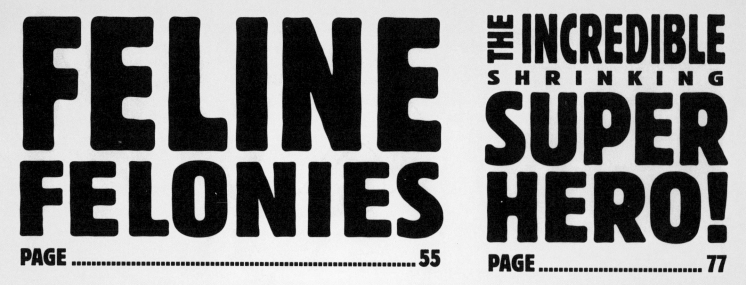

HEROES

SUPERMAN

Sent to Earth from Krypton, Superman was raised as Clark Kent by small-town farmers and taught to value truth and justice. When not saving the world with his super-strength, heat vision, and freezing breath, Clark is a reporter for Metropolis's newspaper, the *Daily Planet*.

WONDER WOMAN

Born on Paradise Island, home of the Amazons, Wonder Woman was given the gifts of great wisdom, strength, beauty, and speed by the ancient Greek gods. Using her Invisible Jet, magic lasso, and unbreakable silver bracelets, she fights for peace and justice. Wonder Woman leads a double life as military intelligence expert Diana Prince.

BATMAN

As a boy, the billionaire Bruce Wayne swore to avenge the deaths of his parents. He spent years mastering all forms of combat and creating an arsenal of cutting-edge equipment. He now fights crime in Gotham City as Batman.

ROBIN

After teenager Tim Drake determined the secret identity of Batman, he underwent months of grueling training to become the Boy Wonder.

ALFRED PENNYWORTH

This loyal butler maintains both Wayne Manor and Batman's secret lair. He also makes a delightful cup of tea.

COMMISSIONER JAMES GORDON

The head of Gotham's police department is a close ally of the Dark Knight.

LOIS LANE

Lois Lane is an award-winning journalist for the *Daily Planet* newspaper. Her biggest scoop was writing about being saved by the mysterious hero of Metropolis and naming him "Superman." Now she competes with reporter Clark Kent to get exclusive stories on the mighty Man of Steel. Little does she know that the two men are one and the same!

VILLAINS

LEX LUTHOR

Lex Luthor is one of the smartest, wealthiest, and most dangerous businessmen in the world. Lex *was* the most powerful man in Metropolis . . . until Superman came along! Now Lex uses his company, LexCorp, to manufacture secret weapons and scientific research in his unending quest to eliminate the Man of Steel.

METALLO

John Corben was a petty thief and con man. After being rescued from a near-fatal car accident, Corben became the test subject for a scientific experiment. His brain was transplanted into the body of a robot named Metallo—a shape-changing criminal cyborg with a heart of kryptonite. His one mission: to destroy Superman!

CATWOMAN

Gotham's resident cat burglar, Catwoman steals from the rich and keeps the loot for herself. She is an expert at hand-to-hand combat, and she uses her claws and whip to pull off her cat-themed capers.

CHEETAH

While searching for ancient treasures to bring herself fame and fortune, archaeologist Dr. Barbara Ann Minerva unleashed a curse that gave her incredible strength and super-speed—and transformed her into the evil Cheetah!

BRAINIAC

From the alien planet of Colu, Brainiac has a brain as powerful as any supercomputer. He travels in his skull-shaped spaceship in his quest to collect shrunken cities and conquer the galaxy.

POISON IVY

A passionate protector of the earth, Poison Ivy is a vigilante for the environment. She uses tactics that are harmful to her fellow humans and is as poisonous as her name suggests. She is immune to all toxins.

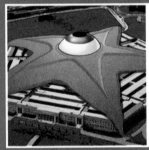

STARRO

An evil starfishlike creature from outer space, Starro controls the minds of others using probes. He will stop at nothing until his mission for universal conquest is complete.

DARKSEID

Supreme ruler of the fiery planet Apokolips, Darkseid is determined to conquer the entire universe. Besides having immense strength and invulnerability, he is able to shoot Omega Beams from his eyes and can travel to different worlds and dimensions using a device known as a Mother Box.

PARASITE

Rudy Jones worked as a janitor at S.T.A.R. Labs until he was exposed to a strange chemical radiation that changed his life. With the ability to absorb bio-energy, Rudy became the super-villain known as Parasite. His constant craving for power will not let him rest until he feasts on Superman and steals all of his amazing abilities!

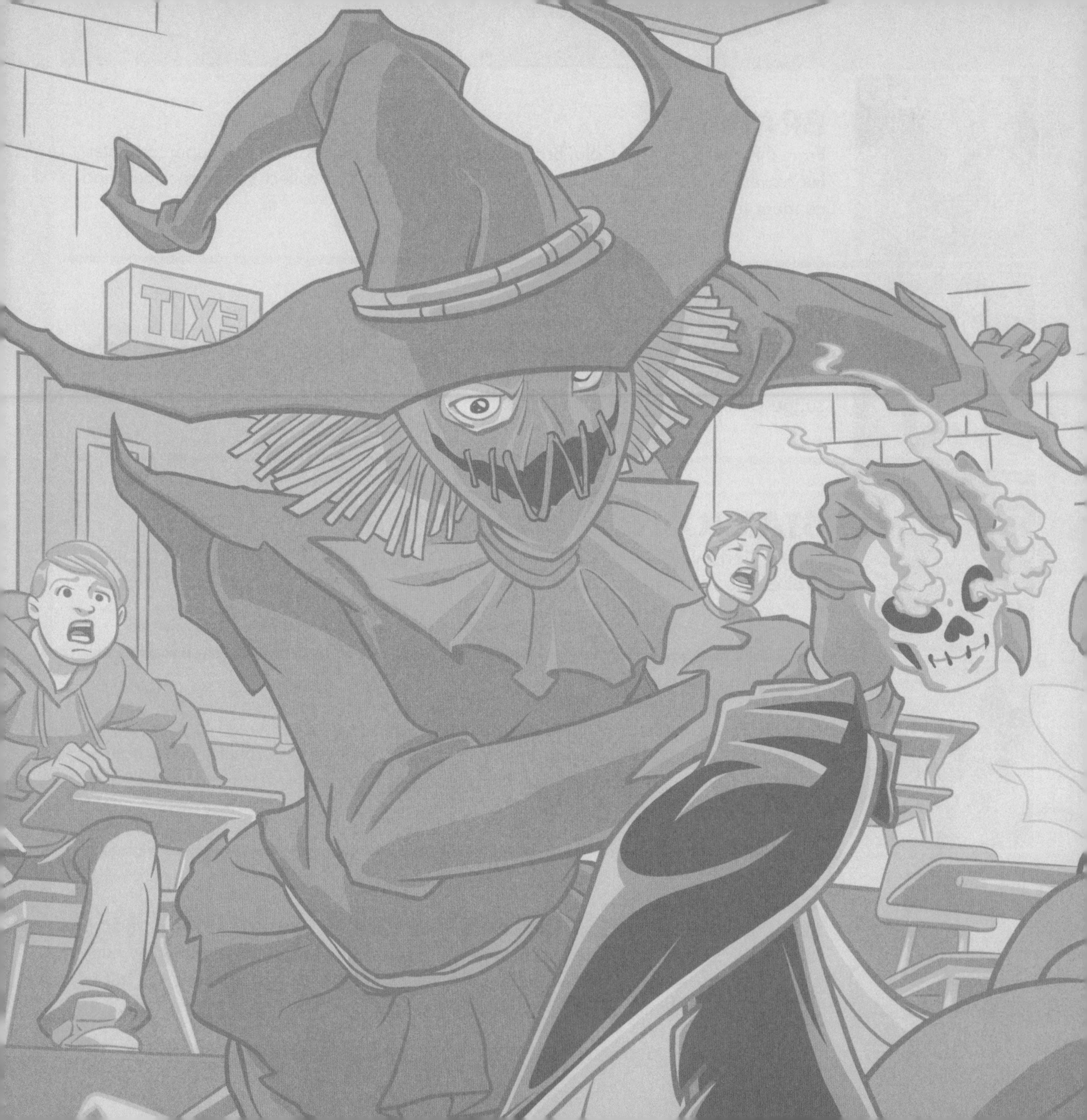

GOTHAM'S VILLAINS UNLEASHED!

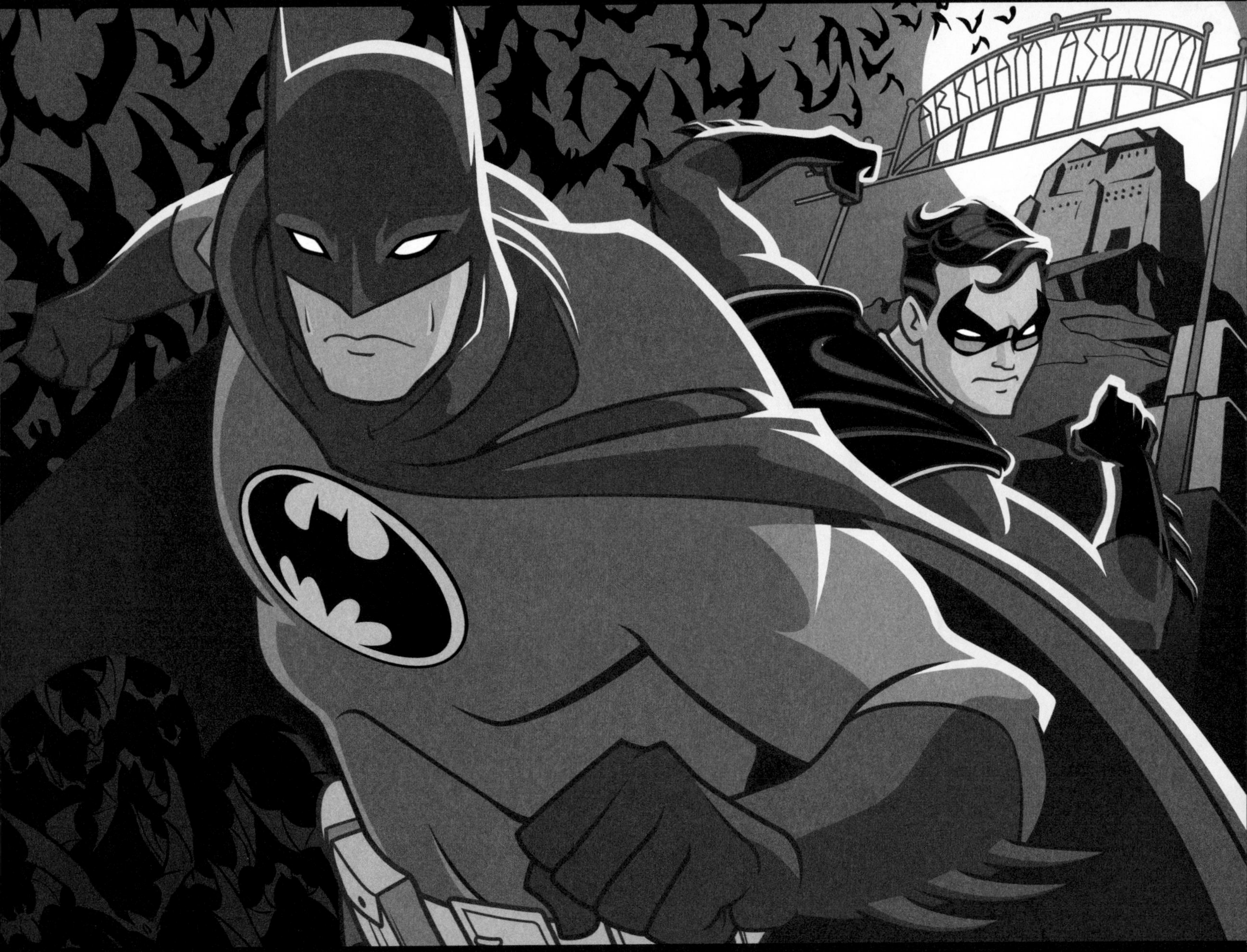
ARKHAM ASYLUM

Protecting Gotham City is a difficult task, so the police need Batman and Robin's help to fight crime. The Dynamic Duo use their gadgets, wits, and strength to keep the city safe.

One day, an alarm sounds throughout the secret, underground Batcave. The Batcomputer relays a terrible message:

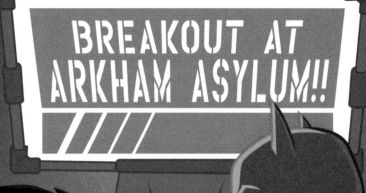

BREAKOUT AT ARKHAM ASYLUM!!

Arkham Asylum houses Gotham's most dangerous villains. That is, until the Joker plays the ultimate prank and busts them loose. The villains can't wait to cause chaos all over the city.

"Now that's a *punch* line!" the crook cackles.

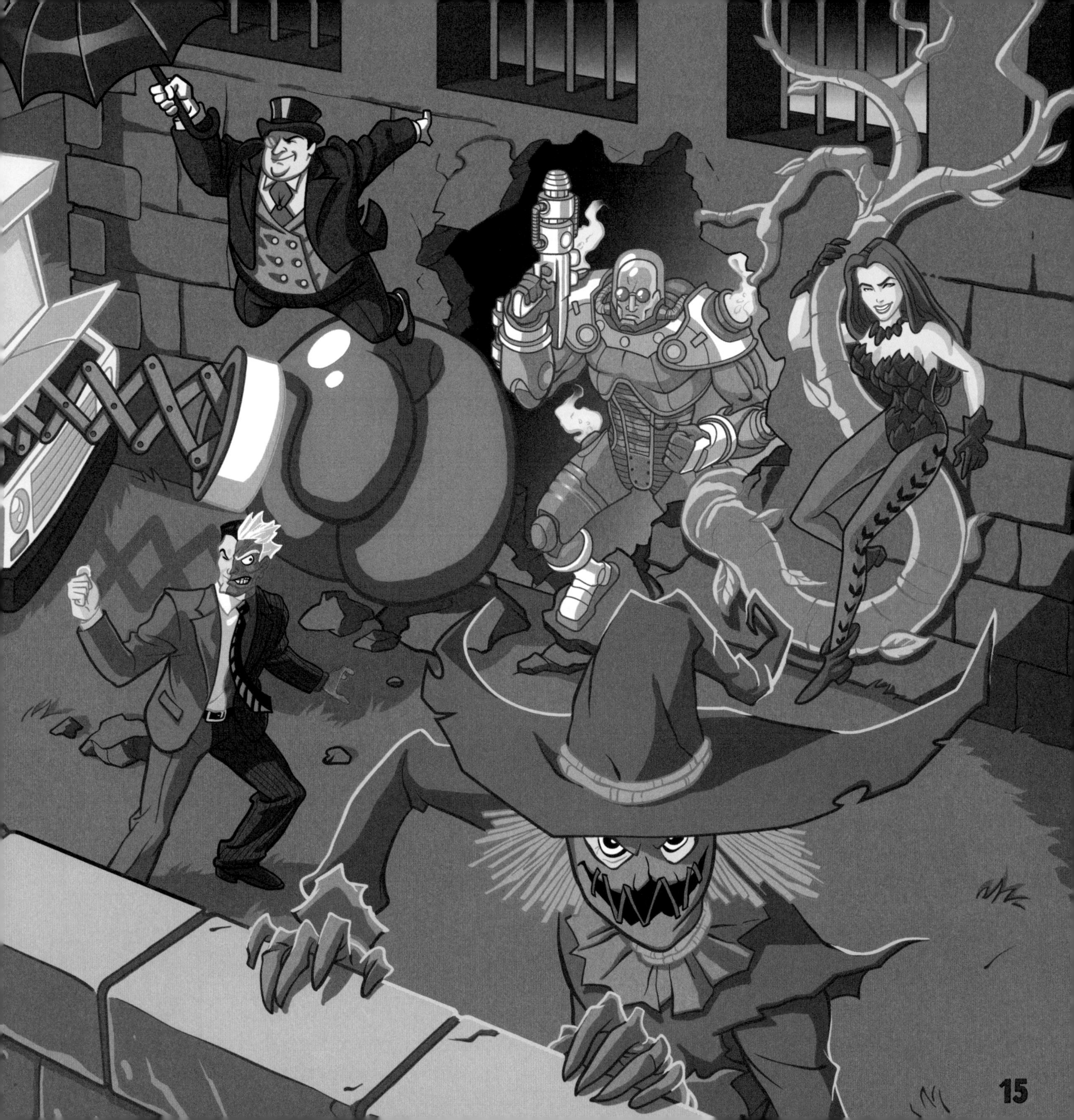

Batman and Robin quickly study their foes to prepare for their mission.

THE PENGUIN Real name: Oswald Chesterfield Cobblepot
Waddles and has beaklike nose • Professional thief • Loves birds
Weapons include trick umbrellas used for flying or fighting

TWO-FACE Real name: Harvey Dent • Once Gotham's District Attorney,
now two men trapped in one body • Courthouse attack deformed half his face
Flips two-headed coin to make decisions for good or evil

POISON IVY Real name: Pamela Isley
A botanist committed to preserving the environment • Has a toxic touch and
immunity to poisons • Has ability to make plants do her bidding

MR. FREEZE Real name: Victor Fries • Scientist frozen during a lab accident
Must wear a suit to keep his body temperature below zero • Turned to a life of
crime to fund his research • Weapons include a freeze gun

THE JOKER Real Name: Unknown • Clownlike appearance caused by
falling into a vat of chemicals • Twisted, dangerous sense of humor • Brilliant
prank engineer • Weapons include deadly versions of party gags

SCARECROW Real name: Jonathan Crane • Once a psychology professor at
Gotham State University • Lost his job when his experiments went too far • Uses a
fear toxin that makes victims experience their worst nightmares

It's time to round up the Rogues!
"To the Batmobile!" the Dark Knight exclaims.
"To the Batcycle," Robin calls out. The Dynamic Duo zoom into action.

Robin speeds away to Gotham State University, where the Scarecrow is threatening to unleash his fear toxin. Robin bursts into a classroom. "Class dismissed!" Robin declares. The Scarecrow pulls out his poison blaster.

Fitted with a gas mask, the Boy Wonder is unaffected by the Scarecrow's fumes. He gives the dangerous doctor a taste of his own medicine.

Across town, Batman arrives at Gotham Park to find that the plant life has taken over. He is quickly caught in Poison Ivy's trap. While the vile villainess laughs, Batman tries desperately to reach the vine-withering spray on his belt.

"Oh, Batman, you look di*vine*!" Poison Ivy cries.

Batman frees himself from the vines and wraps Poison Ivy up in the Batrope!

Batman and Robin's night is far from over. The Penguin is trying to take over the Gotham Zoo!

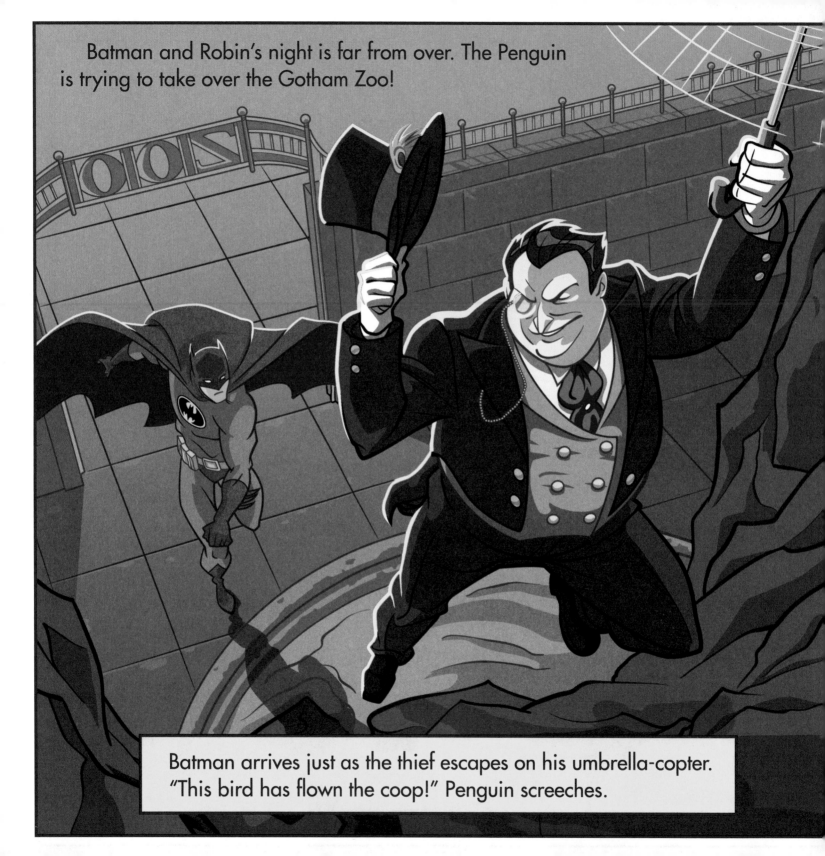

Batman arrives just as the thief escapes on his umbrella-copter. "This bird has flown the coop!" Penguin screeches.

"Time to go back in your cage," orders the Caped Crusader. He straps into his Bat-Glider and takes flight.

Batman uses his grappling hook to ensnare the feathered fink and brings him in for a crash landing.

Meanwhile, Mr. Freeze has turned the Gotham City Diamond Exchange into a block of ice. The villain freezes Robin in his tracks.

Batman follows Robin's distress call to the scene. He sticks an exploding Batarang into the ice wall, and the blast creates an avalanche that covers Mr. Freeze, knocking him out cold. Batman then frees Robin using his Bat-Laser Cutter. "That is so *cool*!" Robin cheers.

When the police arrive to round up Mr. Freeze, Commissioner Gordon has news for Batman.

"Two-Face just robbed the Second National Bank," the policeman says.

"We're on it," Batman replies.

In no time, the Dynamic Duo catches up to Two-Face and his gang. "We've got *double trouble*, boys!" the criminal comments.

Thinking fast, Batman presses the turbo boost button in the Batmobile and slams the getaway van off the road. Robin takes care of the henchmen as Batman confronts Two-Face. "Tell me where the Joker is!" Batman orders. The bank robber flips his coin, and he tells Batman where the Clown Prince of Crime is hiding.

The heroes drive out to the old Funhouse on Gotham Harbor. The Joker flees. "Stay here, Robin. The Joker is a tricky foe!" the Dark Knight commands.

Batman leaps out of the Batmobile and runs after the jeering jester. The chase is on!

Batman follows the Joker's cackle into the Hall of Mirrors. Inside, the Caped Crusader is surrounded by several laughing faces. But which one is the real deal?

"Looks like *this* Joker is *wild*! *Hahahaha!*" the madman screams.

Batman attacks the one Joker different from the others.

The Joker throws an exploding deck of cards at Batman and disappears in a cloud of green smoke. Running out the back exit, the Joker hops onto his Joker Ski, but it won't start! In an instant, the Dark Knight pounces and wipes the smile off the Joker's face.

Outside the Funhouse, Robin is waiting with the police. He holds up the spark plug he removed from the engine in the Joker Ski. "Looks like the joke's on you!" Robin laughs.

As the Joker is led back to Arkham Asylum, the Dynamic Duo prepares for the next mission. "To the Batcave!" Batman and Robin shout together.

SUPERMAN AND THE MAYHEM OF METALLO

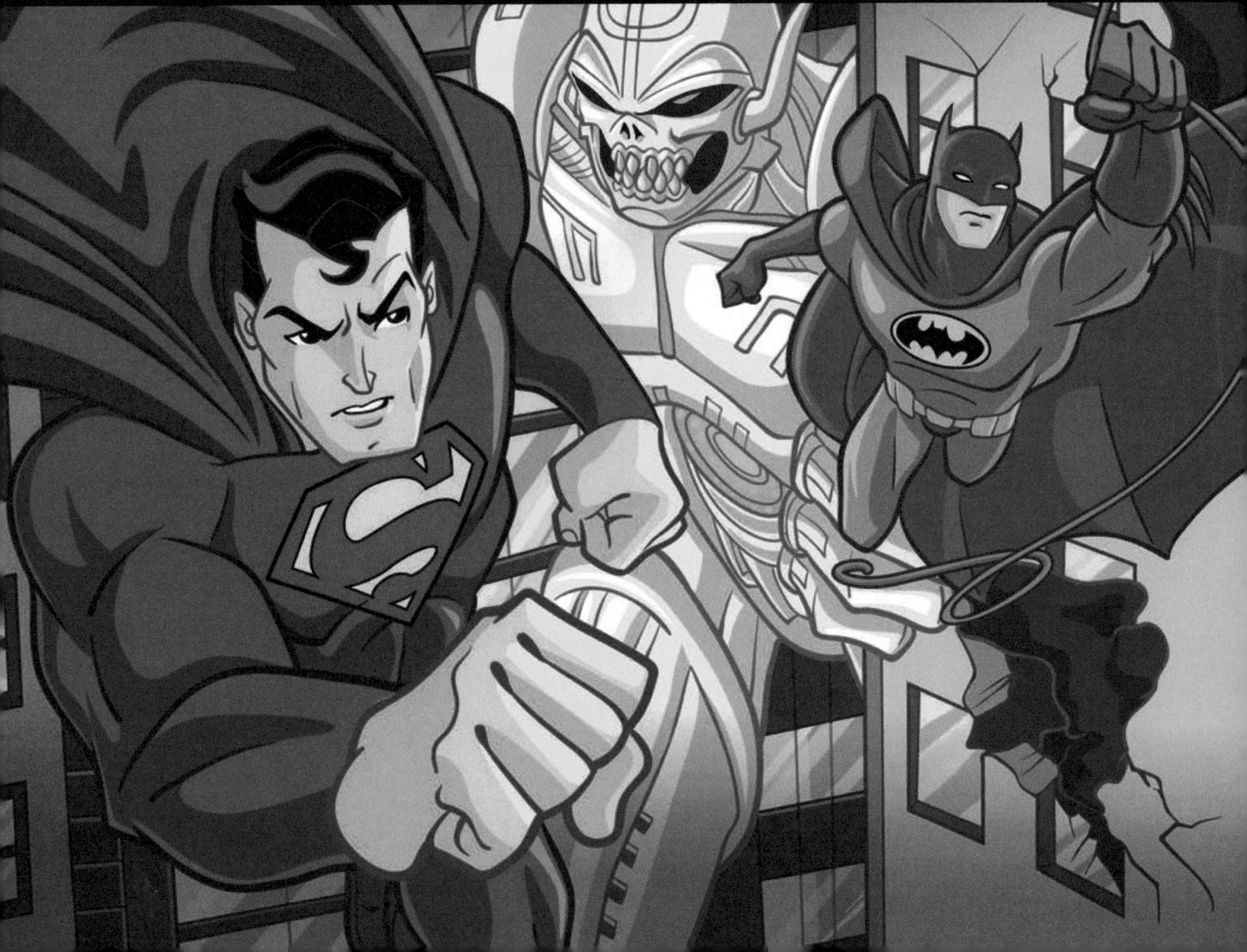

Lex Luthor chuckles as he looks out over Metropolis. The villain wants to get rid of Superman, and Metallo is sure to get the job done! He has the mind of a criminal, the body of a robot, and a heart of kryptonite—a rock from Superman's home planet that drains the hero's powers.

"Show him what you've got,"
Lex says into a radio that transmits
directly to the half-robot, half-man.
"With pleasure!" Metallo laughs.
Within seconds, Metallo is toppling
over buildings and smashing cars.

While working at the Daily Planet building, Clark Kent hears screams from the streets below. He runs to the window and sees Metallo thrashing everything in his path.

"That thing must be stopped before he destroys Metropolis!
This is a job for Superman!"

In a flash, Superman is flying over his beloved city toward the cyborg. *My freezing breath should stop him,* Superman thinks to himself.

Just then, Metallo rips open his chest to reveal his glowing green heart.

"Kryptonite!" Superman gasps.

Metallo slams the weakened Man of Steel with a huge metallic fist. KA-POW!

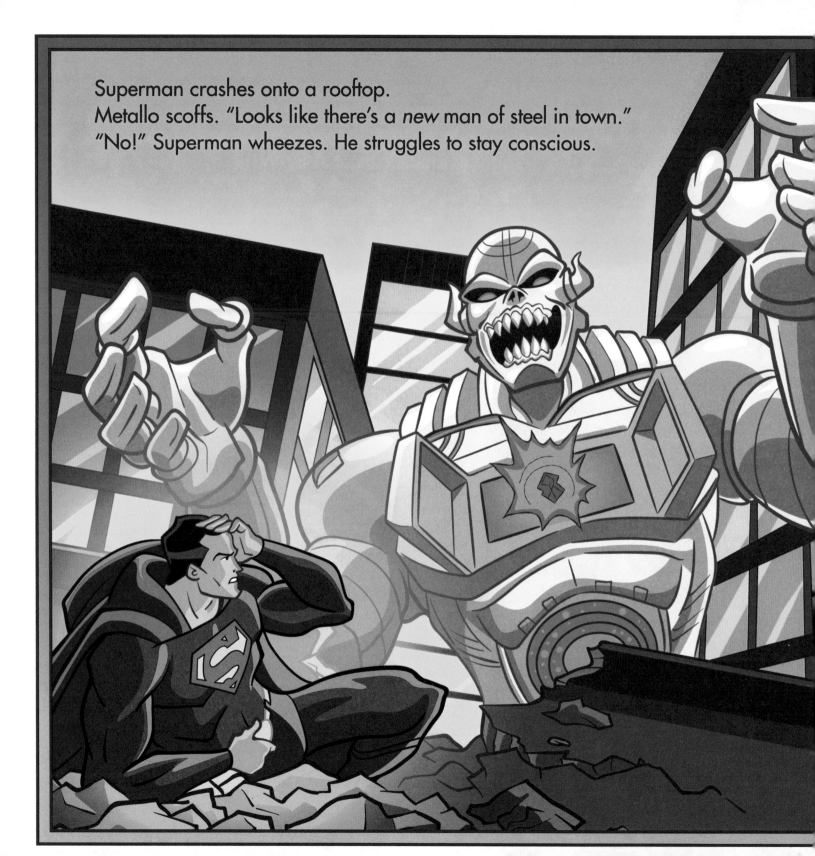

Superman crashes onto a rooftop.
Metallo scoffs. "Looks like there's a *new* man of steel in town."
"No!" Superman wheezes. He struggles to stay conscious.

Suddenly, a dark shadow passes over Superman's face. "Batman!" hisses Lex, watching from the safety of his office building.

LEXCO

Batman positions his Batwing at the metal monster.

"I must get that kryptonite before it destroys Superman," he says. The Batwing dips and loops as Metallo slashes the air. Batman waits patiently for a clear shot . . . and gets it!

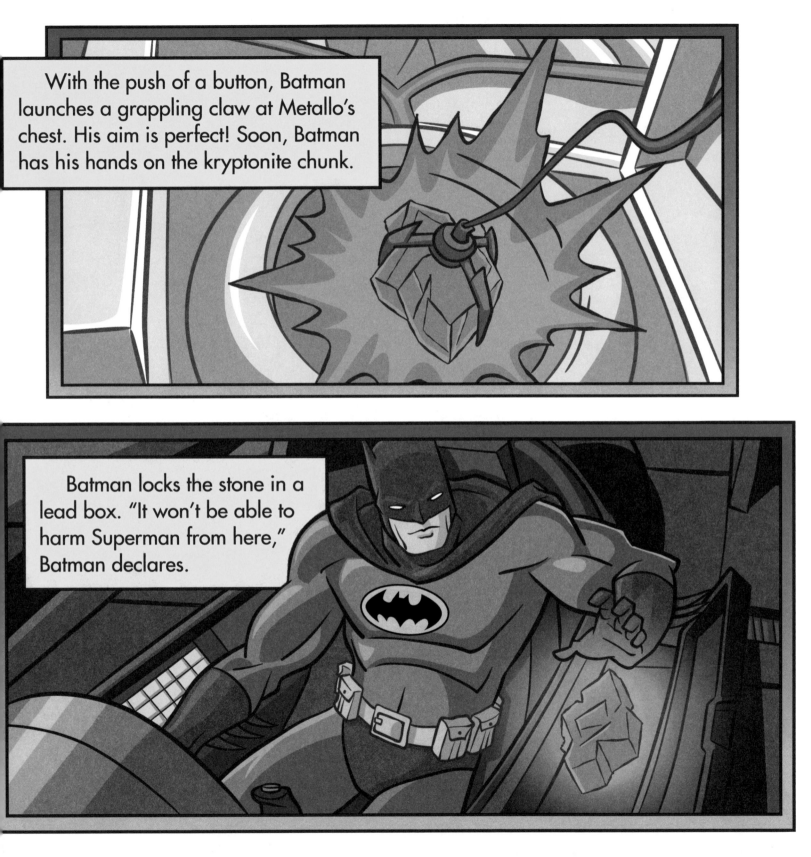

With the push of a button, Batman launches a grappling claw at Metallo's chest. His aim is perfect! Soon, Batman has his hands on the kryptonite chunk.

Batman locks the stone in a lead box. "It won't be able to harm Superman from here," Batman declares.

Furious, Metallo punches at the Batwing, sending it spiraling toward the Daily Planet building. The Dark Knight ejects from the cockpit.
Batman throws flash bombs at the metallic monster, trying to blind him.
"Aah! My eyes!" yells Metallo.

Superman recovers from his haze . . .
just in time to swoop down and catch the
Batwing before it shatters into pieces! He
places it on a nearby rooftop.

"You're not going anywhere," Superman says as he uses his heat vision to melt Metallo's feet into the ground. Blinded and melded to the city streets, Metallo is at a standstill, whining robotically.

Batman realizes he can stop this metal man once and for all. He reaches into his Utility Belt for his Bat-Taser.

The Dark Knight zaps the cyborg. ZZZZZARK!
Metallo collapses into a smoky mess as the electricity
from the Taser shorts out his robotic circuitry.

Then Superman flies the evil hunk of junk into space, where he will no longer be able to harm the good citizens of Metropolis.

Meanwhile, Batman uses his Bat-Tracker to pick up the frequency that controlled Metallo. "Surprise, surprise," Batman says, as he discovers Lex Luthor was behind the robot attack.

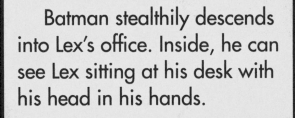

Batman stealthily descends into Lex's office. Inside, he can see Lex sitting at his desk with his head in his hands.

"Looks like Metallo isn't the only monster with a heart of kryptonite," Batman says as he snaps on the Bat-cuffs.

"Blast you, Batman!" Lex snarls.

After bringing Lex to the Metropolis police, Superman flies Batman back to Gotham City inside the damaged Batwing.

"Thank you, friend," says Superman.
"I couldn't have done this without your help."

FELINE FELONIES

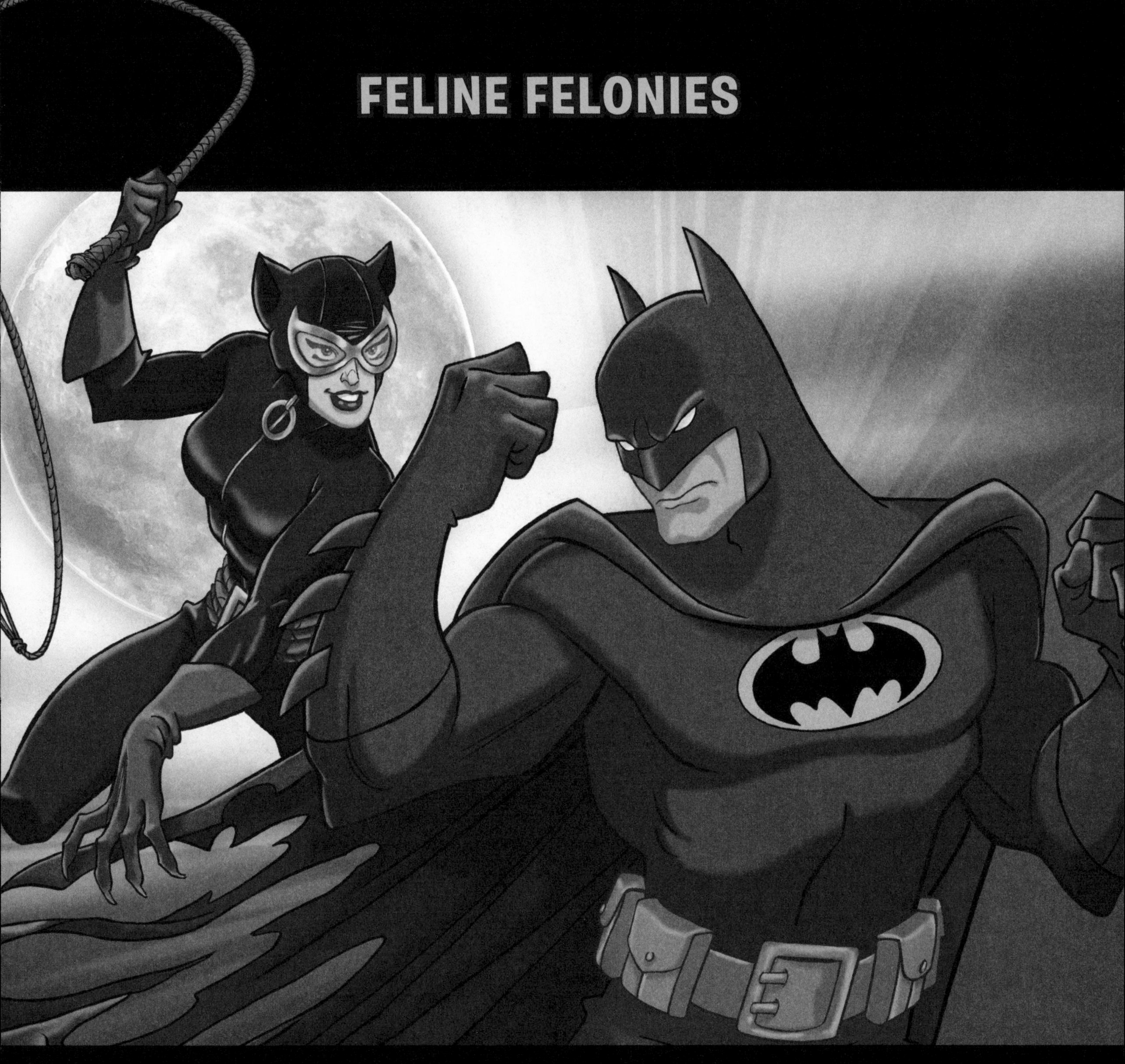

Deep in the night, two dark shadows move across the Gotham City rooftops. One of them is Batman. He follows the trail of an elusive cat burglar to Wayne Towers.

Batman lands on the balcony of the penthouse. In it is the Golden Cat, a statue so rare and valuable few have ever even seen it. Only one thief in Gotham would dare try to pull off such a cat-themed robbery.

"It ends here, Catwoman!" growls the Caped Crusader.

The thief steps into the moonlight. But it's not Catwoman . . . it's the C
Batman is stunned.

"They say you're the world's greatest detective, but I'm not impresse
hisses the feline felon. "Out of my way. I've got a city to rob!"

The Cheetah tries to slash Batman with her sharp claws, but he uses his cape to protect himself.

With catlike speed, the Cheetah leaps off the balcony into the darkness. Batman quickly throws a Bat-Tracker onto the escaping villainess.

The Caped Crusader contacts Wonder Woman from his Batmobile. "Your archenemy almost made me her new scratching post," Batman says. "The Cheetah is in Gotham?" Wonder Woman asks. "I'm on my way!"

Minutes later, Wonder Woman lands her Invisible Jet on the roof of the Gotham City Museum, where Batman is waiting for her.

"My Bat-Tracker led me here," says Batman. "The Cat's Eye Opal is on display and worth millions." "Let's pounce!" Wonder Woman replies.

The Cheetah breaks into the dark museum only to discover that Gotham City's original cat burglar, Catwoman, is already on the scene . . . and she has her paws on the famous gem!

"And who might you be?" Catwoman asks.
"I'm the Cheetah," says the villainess. "And you're stealing my Cat's Eye!"
Catwoman raises her claws and hisses. "Come any closer, and this won't be the only cat's eye you lose!"
"Mee-ouch!" the Cheetah snaps back.

The night watchmen hear the catfight and sound the alarm.

"Time to crash this party!" Batman says.

"Look what the Cheetah dragged in!" Catwoman snarls.
The Caped Crusader and the Amazon Princess face off against their feline foes.
The cat burglars have to work together to get out of this tight spot.

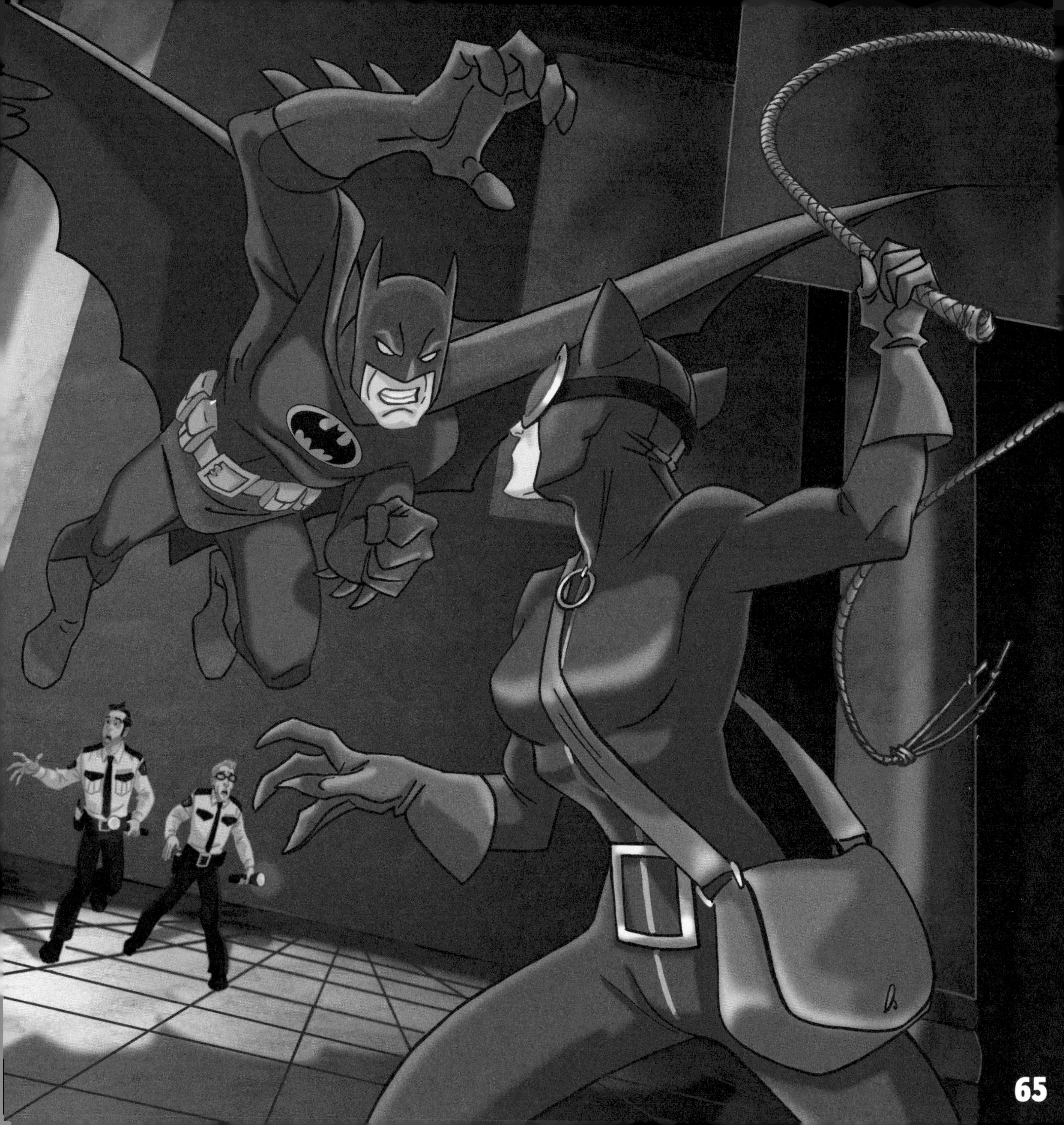

The Cheetah and Catwoman grab the guards and take them hostage.
"Not another step," the Cheetah yells.
"Or else!" Catwoman finishes.
The heroes must allow the criminals to go, in order to save the hostages.

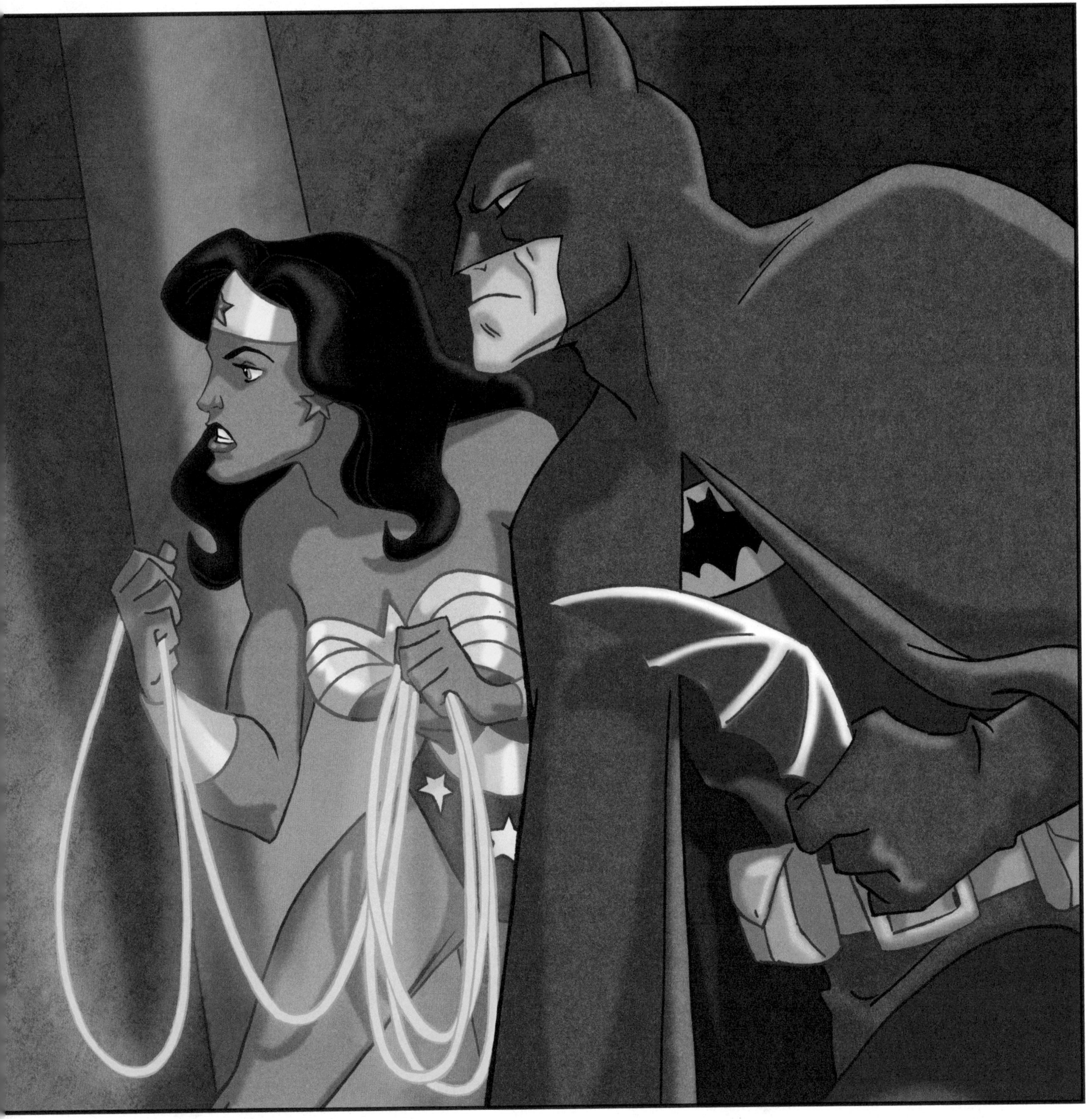

Back on the roof, Batman is angry at this turn of events.

"We can still find them with your Bat-Tracker," Wonder Woman says.

"That's true," says Batman. "I have a plan." He looks at the Invisible Jet and smiles. "They won't know what hit them!"

Across town, Catwoman and the Cheetah are now working together to steal the white tiger from the Gotham City Zoo.

"Such a beautiful and powerful creature does not belong in a cage," Catwoman purrs.

"Let's train her to do our bidding!" the Cheetah exclaims.

As Catwoman picks the lock, she is startled by a flying Batarang. The felines scan the darkness but the heroes are nowhere to be seen.

"Show yourself, Batman!" says Catwoman. "I know you found us with some sort of Bat-gadget."

"I bet they're hiding in that blasted Invisible Jet," the Cheetah warns.

"Not anymore," says a voice. Wonder Woman appears behind the Cheetah and knocks her to the ground.

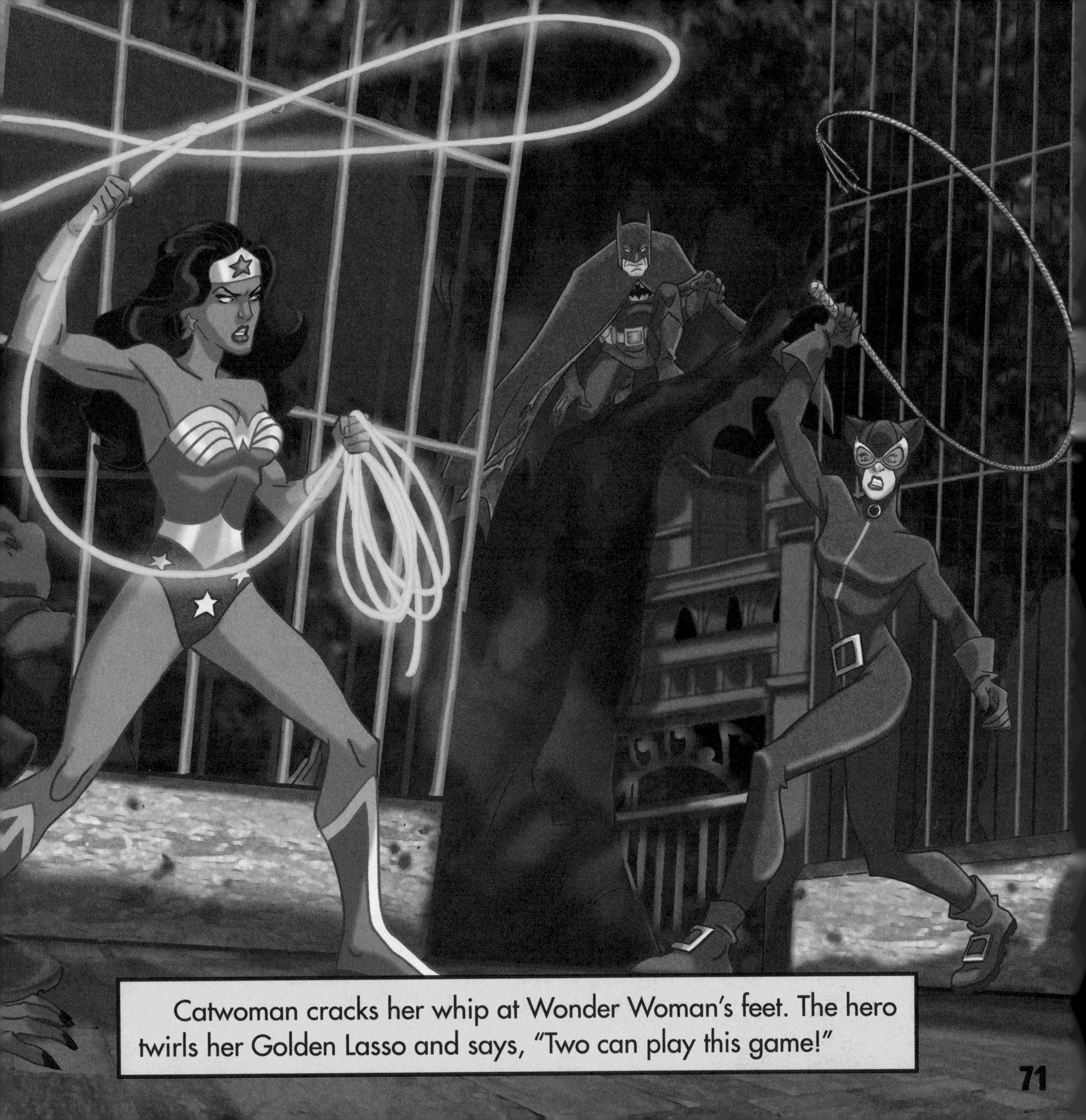

Catwoman cracks her whip at Wonder Woman's feet. The hero twirls her Golden Lasso and says, "Two can play this game!"

The battle is fierce, but Catwoman is no match for the Amazon Princess. She uses her unbreakable lasso to tie up the burglar.

Meanwhile, the Cheetah runs into the lion den. The Caped Crusader emerges from the shadows and swings high overhead. He won't let her get away again.

Batman lands in front of the scoundrel, blocking her escape. The great cats come to her aid and surround Batman.

"Ready for round two?" the Cheetah asks, and prepares to strike.

This time, Batman is faster than the Cheetah. He throws a smoke bomb, releasing a cloud of sleeping gas. When the air clears, *all* the felines are taking a catnap.

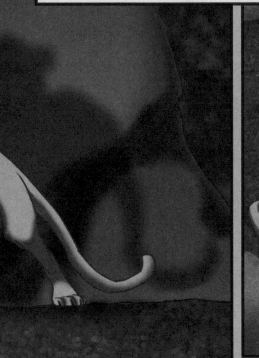

Wonder Woman ties the two crooks together while Batman calls the police.
"It's time to put these kittens in a cage," Wonder Woman says.
"There's a big one nearby called Gotham State Prison," Batman replies.
76 "It's cat-proof!"

THE INCREDIBLE SHRINKING SUPER HERO!

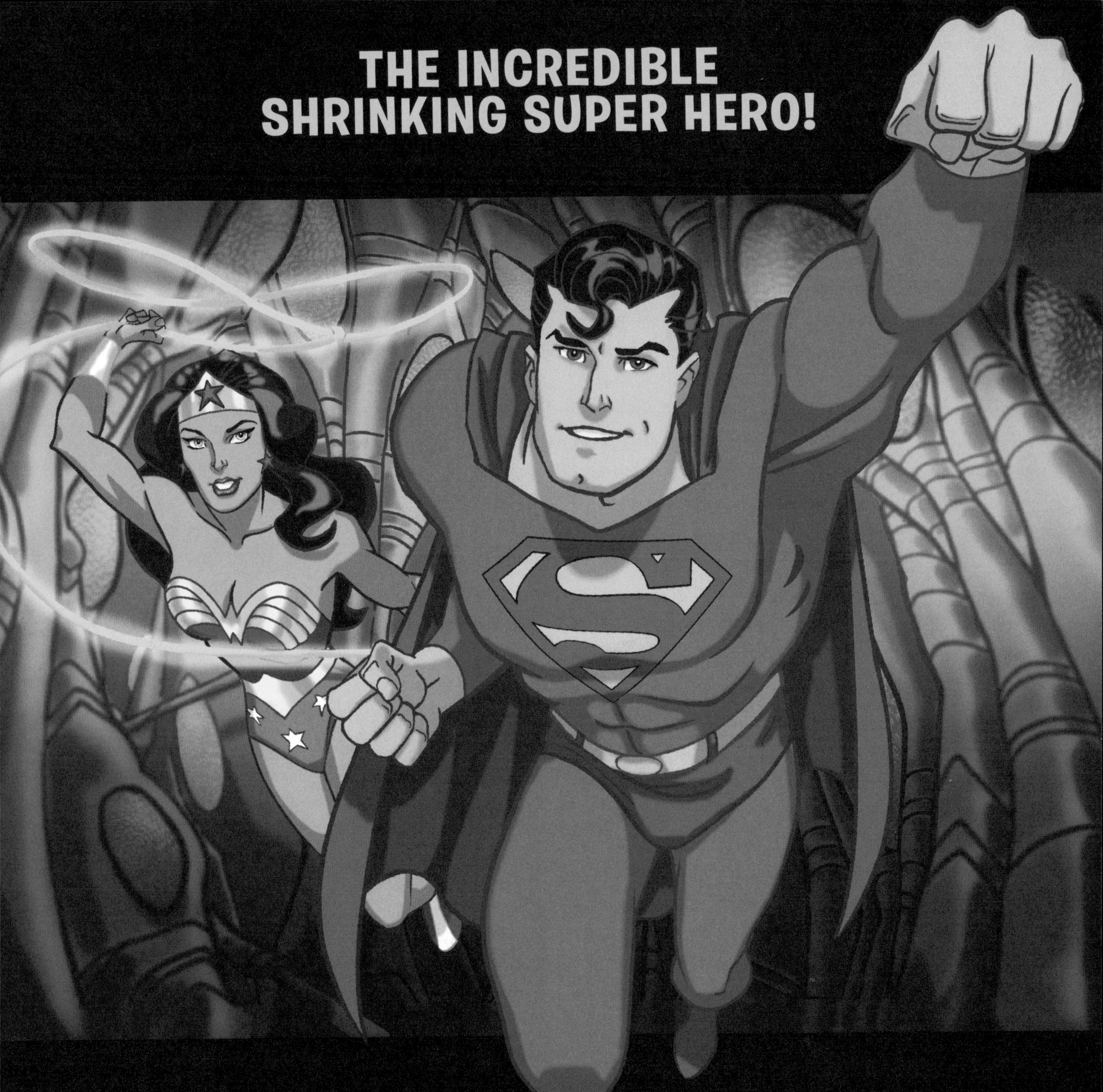

It's a sunny day in Washington, DC. The president of the United States of America is about to award Superman and Wonder Woman the highest honor he can bestow.

"Ladies and gentlemen," says the president, "we are here today to honor two amazing heroes."

"Superman and Wonder Woman's work for justice, peace, and freedom are unmatched here on Earth, if not in the entire galaxy," he continues. "For your service to the nation and to the world, I present you both with the Congressional Medal of Honor."

Suddenly, Superman sees a familiar sight as a golden glow shimmers before him and an old enemy appears. It's the evil alien Brainiac! His mind works like a supercomputer—he is a cunning foe. "I am offended you didn't invite me to such an important event,

"Brainiac!" shouts Wonder Woman. "Not you again!" She pulls out her lasso and prepares to toss it.

"You shouldn't have come back to Earth," says Superman. He jumps in front of the president to protect him.

"I deserve an award, too!" shouts Brainiac. "I think I will add Washington, DC, to my collection of tiny cities—and the president will be a bonus!"

Brainiac aims his shrink ray at the White House and fires.

Wonder Woman crosses her silver bracelets to create a protective shield. She closes her eyes as she struggles against the force of the shrink ray and calls out to Superman, "You have to protect the president!"

But when Wonder Woman opens her eyes, she realizes that Superman and the president have been shrunk! As she reaches out to help them, BraFiniac hits her with his ray gun.

Brainiac teleports all of them to his spaceship. "Superman and the president have become part of my collection, and soon I will shrink Wonder Woman, too," he says with a laugh.

When Wonder Woman wakes up, her arms are secured with steel bands. She quickly tears them apart. Brainiac has underestimated her strength.
She sees that Superman and the president are trapped inside a glass jar with the White House.

Wonder Woman peers into the jar. "Superman, can you hear me?" she asks. She hears a tiny voice reply.

"You have to turn off the force field," yells Superman as he tries to punch the sides of the jar. Wonder Woman finds the right button and disables the force field.

Superman smashes his way out and tells the president to stay put. Then he flies up to Wonder Woman's shoulder.

"Brainiac's force field surrounds this spaceship," he tells her. "We need to destroy his belt buckle to deactivate it and escape."

"I'll worry about him," says Wonder Woman. "You take care of the belt."

87

The heroes find Brainiac in the command center of the ship. "Wonder Woman!" he cries. "You escaped. Well, this won't take long." "No, it won't," says Wonder Woman as she quickly ties up the villain with her Lasso of Truth.

Superman flies straight toward Brainiac and crunches the alien's belt buckle with both fists. Brainiac frees himself— but too late! The force field is already shut down!

Brainiac yells in rage. "How dare you, mini-man!"

"It doesn't matter how big I am. I am still Superman!" says the Man of Steel. He attacks Brainiac, knocking the alien off balance. But Brainiac recovers and laughs. "Is that all you can muster, Superman? You will need more than that!"

Then Brainiac hurls Wonder Woman across the room, where she crashes into the ship's controls!

WARNING

DANGER

"Warning! Ship will lose orbit in sixty seconds," blares the ship's computer.

Wonder Woman's fall damaged the ship's control panel. They are going to crash back to Earth if the heroes don't do something!

Wonder Woman springs back into action and hits Brainiac with all her Amazon might, knocking him to the floor.

Superman grabs the golden lasso and zips around and around Brainiac until he is all tied up!

Wonder Woman grabs the shrink ray gun. She hits the reverse button and fires it at Superman. The Man of Steel quickly grows back to his normal size.

"*Warning! Unable to maintain orbit. All systems failing,*" warns the computer.

Superman seizes the opportunity to finish the villain for good.
He uses his heat vision to blast Brainiac's supercomputer brain!

"Can't think . . . !" says the alien.
"What have you done to me?!"
"The ship will burn up on reentry!"
says Superman. "I'll try to guide it
from outside."
Wonder Woman nods. "Good Luck!"

The heroes hurtle toward Earth. Superman uses his super-strength to slow down the ship, but will it be enough to keep his friends inside safe?

Superman brings the ship in for a perfect landing. He places it gently on the White House lawn.

There is a loud crash as Wonder Woman rips the spaceship door open. She emerges with the precious cargo in tow. The president and the White House are safe!

Moments later the heroes restore the president and the White House to their original sizes. Two secret service men haul Brainiac away to a special holding cell. "Superman and Wonder Woman, I believe these belong to you," says the president as he hands over two medals. "Thank you for your bravery!"

"All in a day's work, Mr. President!" says Superman.

BATMAN AND THE TOXIC TERROR

Claire Cameron - GNN

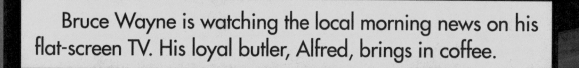

Bruce Wayne is watching the local morning news on his flat-screen TV. His loyal butler, Alfred, brings in coffee.

"Happy Earth Day, Gotham City," Claire Cameron, a perky newscaster, chirps on-screen. "I'm coming to you live from Harris Park. Today this piece of nature will be bulldozed to make way for a brand-new shopping mall." Bruce can't believe his eyes or his ears!

He's not the only one. "My park! My festival of foliage! What are those people *doing*?" Poison Ivy screams.

Claire Cameron - GNN

"If Gotham's politicians have their way, soon every square block will be a somber slab of concrete. I have to stop them!"
Poison Ivy leaps from her perch and begins planning her attack.

Back at Wayne Manor, Bruce makes some calls. "Why is precious green space being sacrificed for yet another mall?" Bruce asks the mayor. "Some of these trees are hundreds of years old!"

"We interrupt our regularly scheduled programming to bring you this breaking story. In a mysterious turn of Earth Day events," the reporter states, "people are turning into trees."

Bruce and Alfred watch scene after horrifying scene of innocent Gotham citizens standing, their legs rooted into the ground like tree trunks, their arms stiff as branches.

"There's only one person capable of this—Poison Ivy!" Bruce yells.

Bruce races to the secret lair beneath Wayne Manor, where he changes into his alter ego, Batman. His suit, weapons, and vehicles stand at the ready.

Meanwhile, Poison Ivy is on a rampage, spraying a noxious toxin throughout the city. She's about to turn some construction workers into plants.

Batman zooms into downtown Gotham, passing dozens of people who have been turned into trees. Block after city block, they stand frozen in conversation, checking watches, sipping coffee.

Pulling to a screeching halt at Harris Park, Batman finds two scared but determined park rangers.

"She ran *that* way," the tall one yells, pointing.

What are you up to now, Poison Ivy? Batman wonders.

Following the ranger's tip, Batman uses his razor-sharp Batarang to rip apart the thickets and tangled vines before him. In only a few short hours, Poison Ivy has turned a friendly park into an impenetrable jungle.

From high above, Poison Ivy watches. She knew that Batman would appear, and was ready for him. "Congratulations! You've made it through the maze. Here is your prize," she exclaims.

Suddenly, Batman is ambushed by two mutant tree people.
He realizes they are the poor park rangers transformed by Ivy's toxins.
Batman must act fast before Ivy runs away.

"You Gothamites think you can do whatever you want to the earth," Poison Ivy hisses.

"The city will be better off with all the people gone and trees taking their place. And that is *exactly* what will happen."

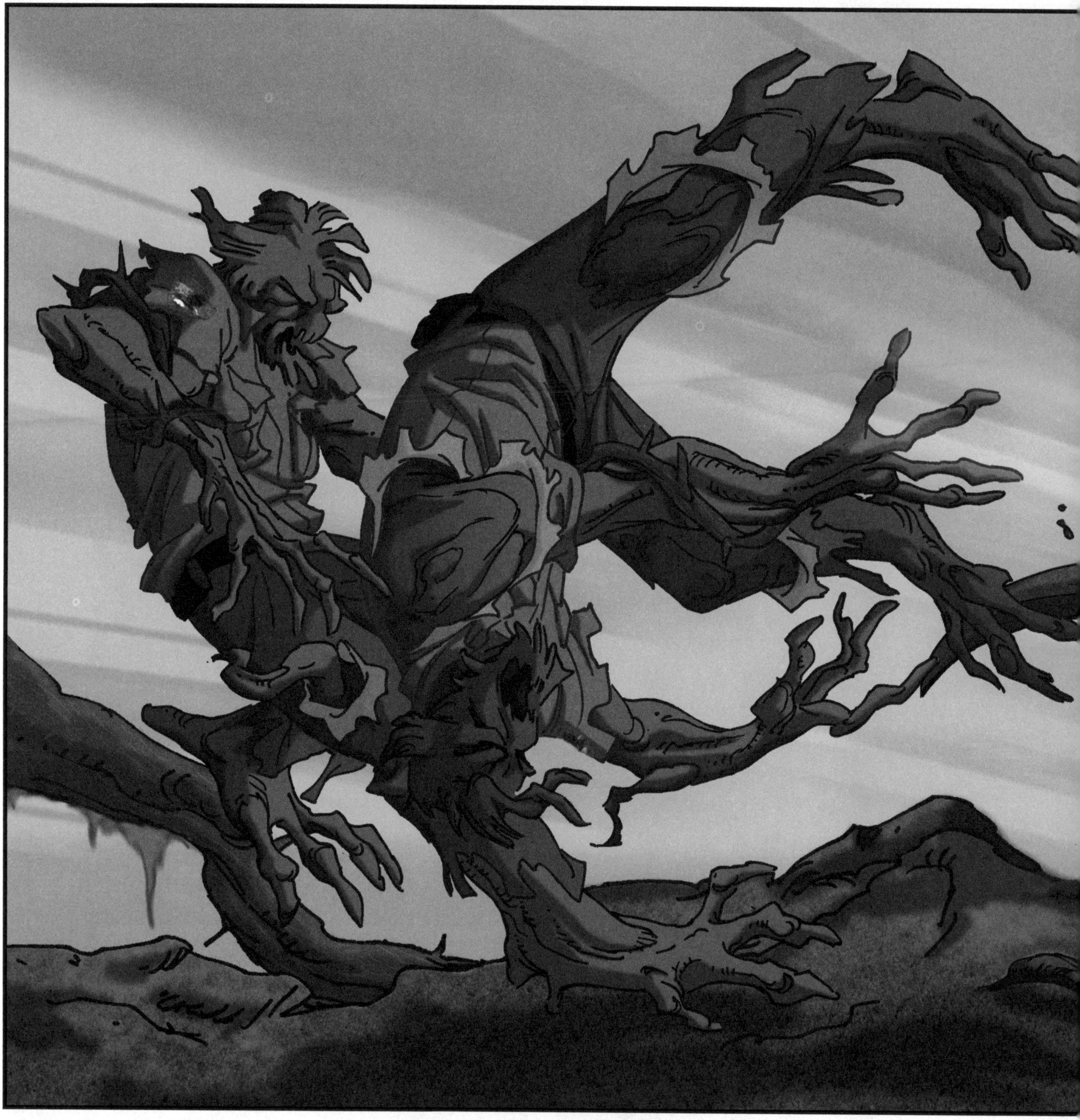

"I don't think so. I'm going to uproot this evil scheme."
Before the villain can get away, Batman uses his lightning-fast reflexes to get out of the guards' hold.

"I will finish the job! You cannot stop me!" she calls, desperately searching for an escape route, as Batman tangles her in his Batrope.

"There are safer ways to protect the environment, Ivy!" Batman scolds her.

While the police take Poison Ivy to headquarters, Batman speeds back to the Batcave to produce an antidote.

Batman sprays the entire city with his Bat-Glider. Slowly the trees become human again. They shed their branches. They scratch their heads with fingers—not twigs!

Before long Gotham is back to normal!

Back at Wayne Manor, Bruce watches the local news.

"Thanks to a generous donation by Wayne Enterprises, today we turn Harris Park into a forest reserve for all the people of Gotham to enjoy for generations!" the mayor declares.

"So long, mall," says Bruce, chuckling.

STARRO AND STRIPES FOREVER

Bruce Wayne's martial arts training is interrupted by startling news.

"This is a breaking story, direct from the Oval Office. The president of the United States demands a Declaration of Independence from super heroes today, the Fourth of July. The nation will no longer accept their assistance in fighting crime. Any future super hero activities have been outlawed."

LIV

BREAKING NEW

SUPER HERO MENACE?
LIVE FROM WHITE HOUSE

Bruce is suspicious. As Batman, he boards the Batplane. He flicks several switches and is boosted with faster-than-light speed to Washington, DC.

In the White House briefing room, Clark Kent is reporting on the staggering story for the *Daily Planet* newspaper. His friend Diana Prince, a government employee, sits with him.

Clark scans the room with his powerful X-ray vision. He discovers a Starro probe on t president's neck! The leader of the free world is controlled by alien foe Starro the Conqu

Knowing something sinister is behind the president's shocking announcement, Clark and Diana race outside. Clark changes into his alter ego, Superman, as Diana whirls to transform herself into Wonder Woman.

The three heroes race to the briefing
room, desperate to save the president.
"Mr. President, you're in danger!"
Superman shouts.

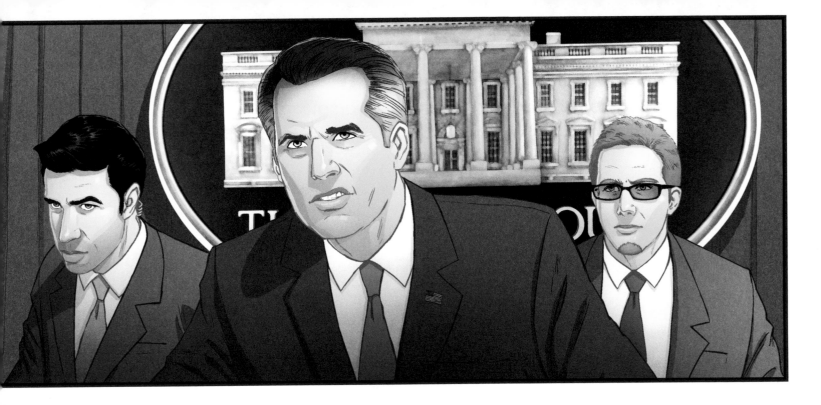

The president instructs his Secret Service agents to arrest Superman, Wonder Woman, and Batman. The agents are under Starro's control, too!

Superman grabs two agents as Wonder Woman ties the rest together with her Golden Lasso.

"You'll thank me for this later," Wonder Woman says.

Meanwhile, Batman leaps into action, trying to remove the Starro probe on the back of the president's neck.

The president, filled with the intergalactic strength of Starro, lifts Batman into the air. Wonder Woman flings her golden tiara at the commander-in-chief, knocking the star from his neck. He and Batman tumble to the floor.

As the president regains his senses, Superman looks out the window to see Starro the Conqueror moving across the sky. The Man of Steel races to catch the giant villain.

As Batman and Wonder Woman remove the probes from the confused Secret Service agents, military helicopters swoop around Superman on all sides, firing lasers at him.

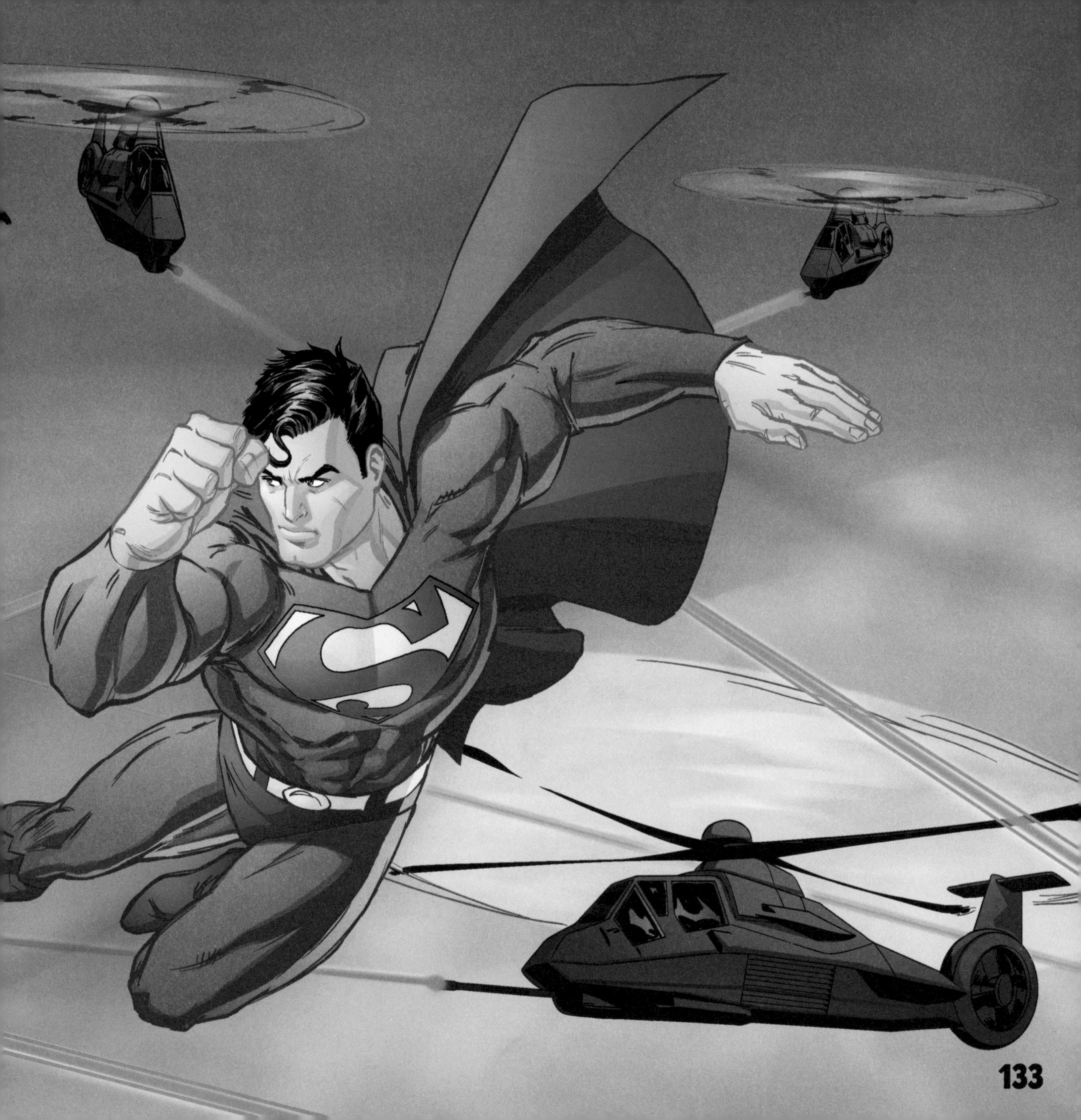

Superman reaches the Pentagon. He finds that Starro has latched itself onto the roof of the famous five-cornered military headquarters.
"Not only is Starro now controlling the military," Superman says, "it's also absorbing the country's secret military intelligence for its future evil plans."

With a great gust of his super-breath, he keeps the helicopters away. Now Superman must battle Starro. But he needs help! He sends a signal with his comm-link.

Batman takes to the sky in his Batplane. Wonder Woman flies next to him in her Invisible Jet.

At the Pentagon, Superman has been using his heat vision on Starro to stop it from carrying out its evil plans.

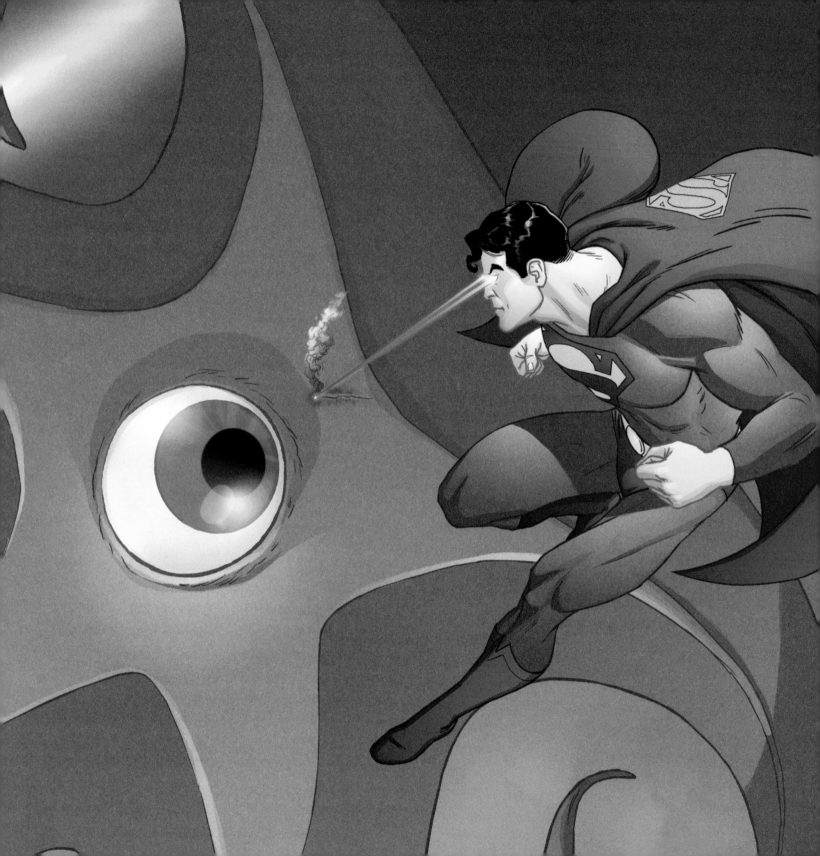

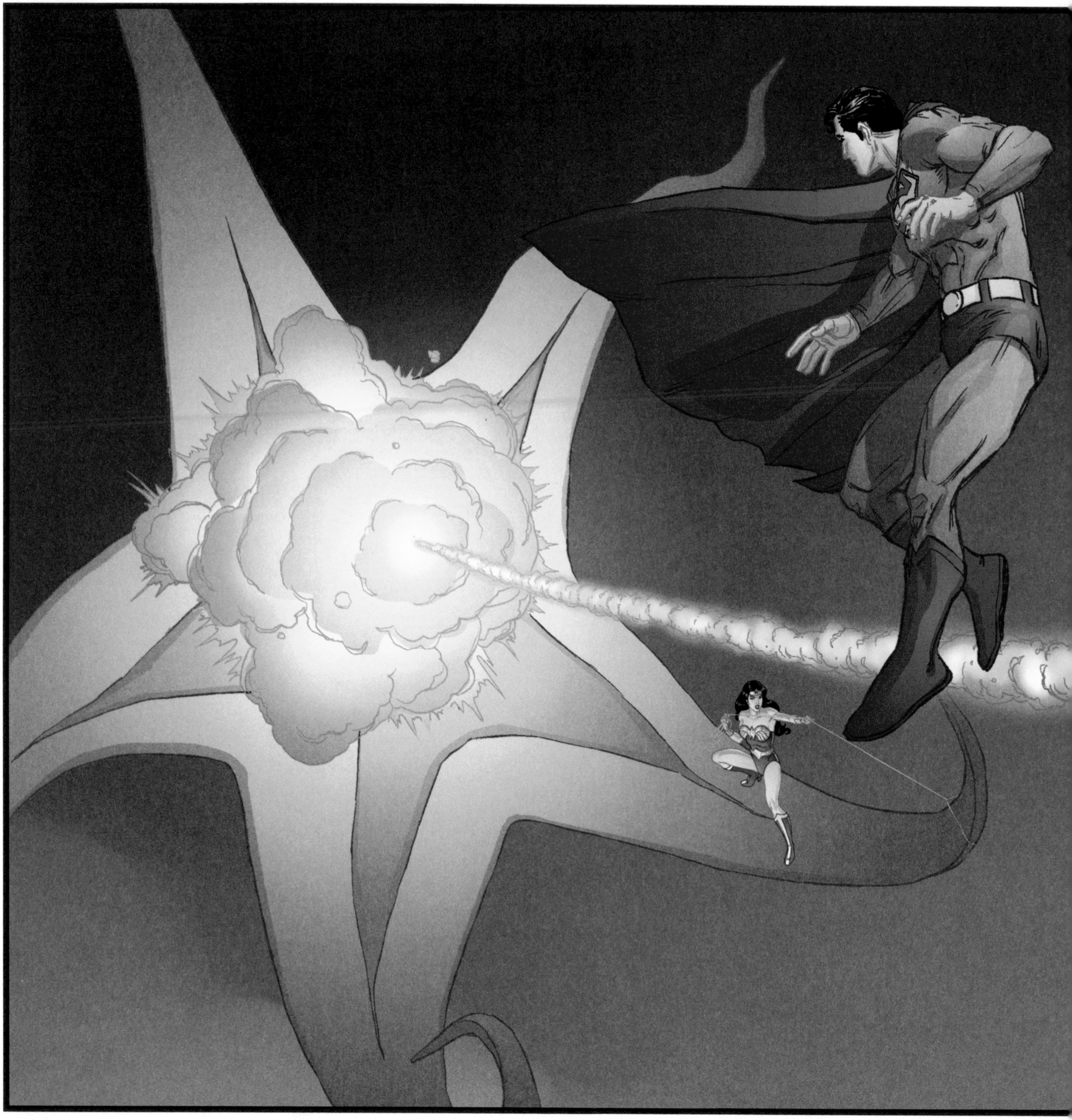

Wonder Woman flings her Golden Lasso down, wrapping it around one of Starro's gigantic arms. Batman pilots his Batplane just above the great starfish and fires a missile at Starro, stunning it.

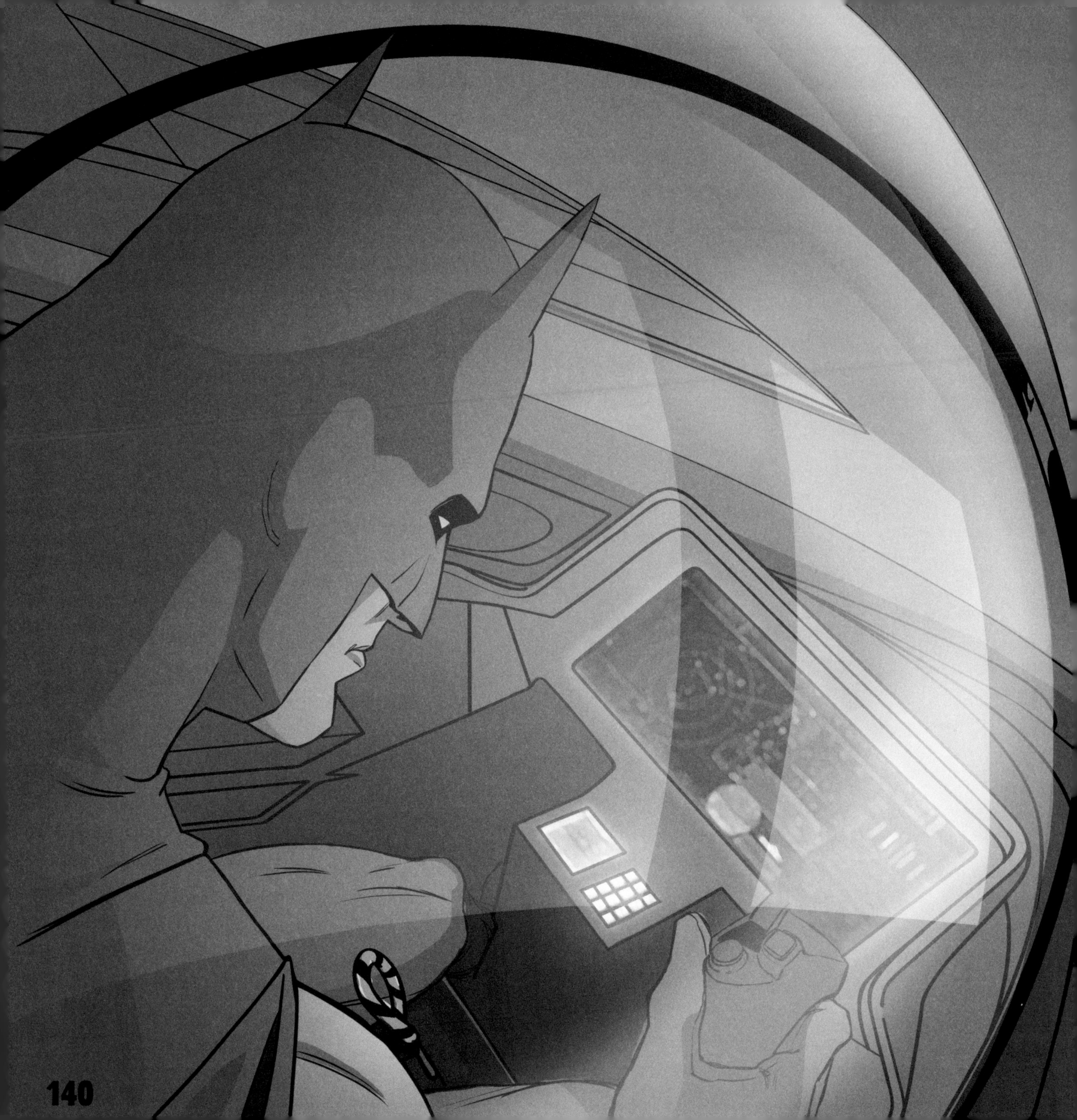

With Starro weaker now, Batman is able to use his shrink-ray to reduce Starro to the size of an ordinary starfish. Superman zooms into space with the villain.

With Starro defeated, the men and women of the military are finally free of its mind control.

141

Back at the White House, Superman, Wonder Woman, and Batman enjoy the fireworks with the president and his family.

"Thanks to the three of you, America today can still celebrate its freedom," the president says. "Happy Fourth of July!"

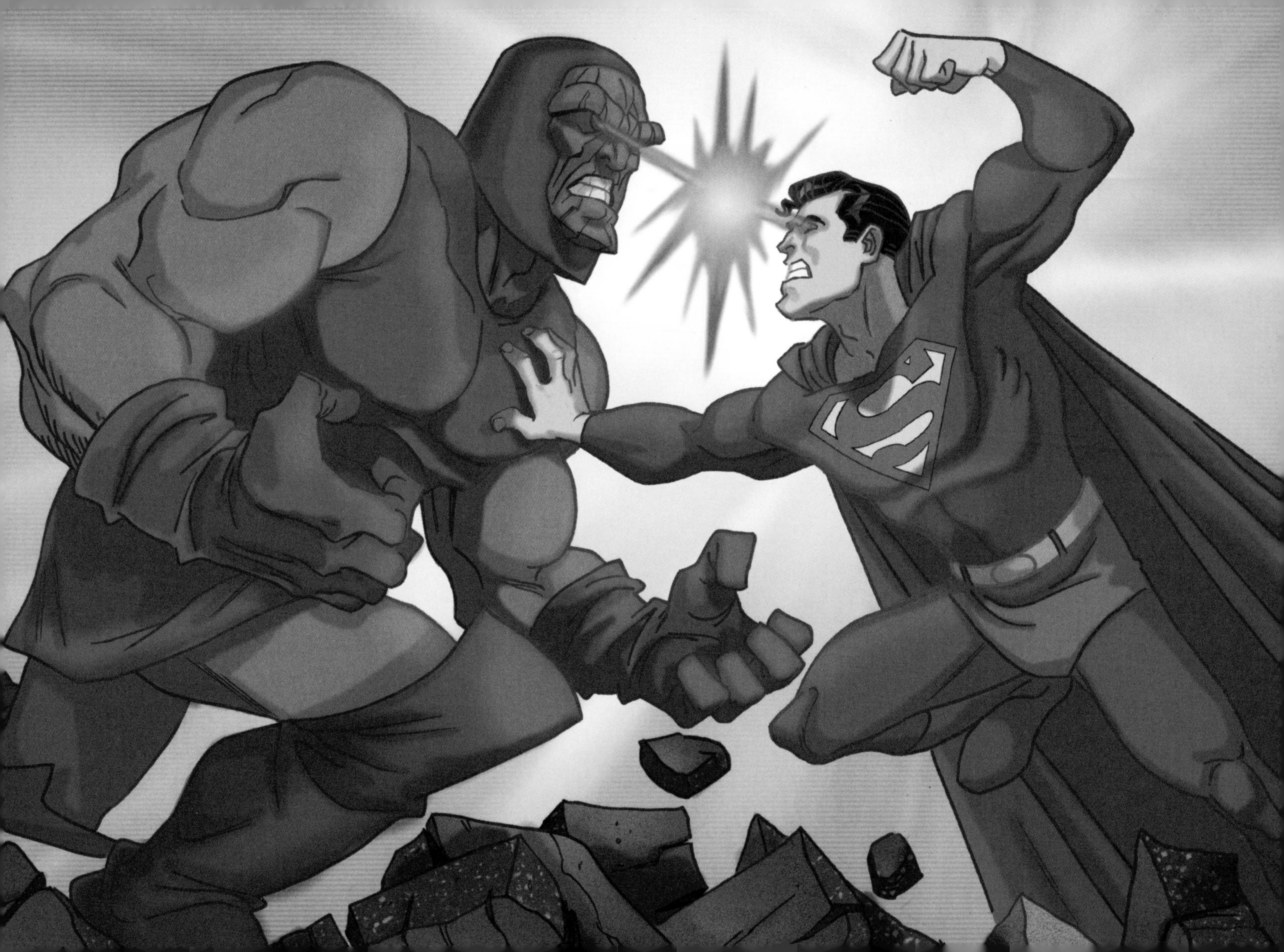

It is another beautiful day in Metropolis. But high up in the Daily Planet building, someone is about to make a horrible discovery.

Jimmy Olsen, young photojournalist, is using his telephoto lens to scan the city streets below for a story.

"Lois," he yells in panic. "Come quick!"

"I'm standing right next to you, Jimmy," says Lois Lane, prizewinning reporter for the *Daily Planet*.

Jimmy passes the camera over to Lois.

"Darkseid." Lois gasps. "You keep snapping pictures. This story could wreck us all."

"Wait, Lois!" says Jimmy. He sees a blur of blue and red beside Darkseid. "He's here! Superman is here!"

"I just hope he can stop that fiend," says Lois. "Do we have any binoculars around here?"

"Welcome, Kal-El, son of Krypton," murmurs Darkseid. His voice is low, but it echoes across downtown.

"Get out of Metropolis, Darkseid," says Superman. "You don't belong here. Go back to Apokolips now."

"Nor do you belong here, Kal-El," says Darkseid. "I'm tired of your misplaced pride in this ridiculous planet. You will destroy this city for me— TODAY!—while the earthlings watch in horror."

"Not a chance," says Superman, launching himself at Darkseid.

With a massive red blast, Darkseid releases Omega Beams from his eyes, sending Superman sprawling.

"I've modified my Omega Beams, son of Krypton. Feel how they wash through your brain," says Darkseid. "You serve *me* now."

"Say it," says Darkseid. "Life and hope are useless."

"Life and hope are useless," repeats Superman, stumbling to his feet.

"Now destroy this useless city," says Darkseid. "And mourn inside as you tear your adopted planet to shreds. Together we will rebuild it in Apokolips's image."

"Yes, my liege," says Superman.

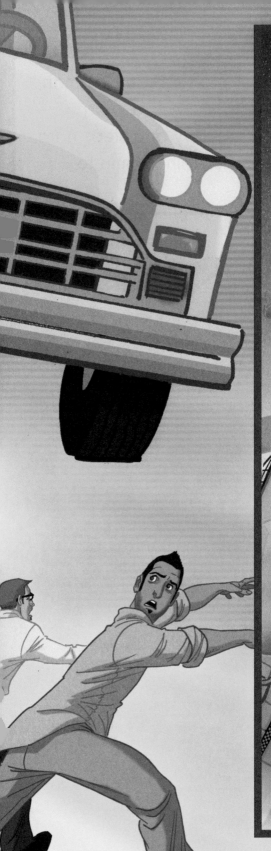

Wonder Woman is soaring over the city in her Invisible Jet when a car comes hurtling past. She quickly locks it in her tractor beams so it won't fall.

"Superman? But why? How?"

As Wonder Woman dives toward the streets to protect Metropolis from its own protector, she sends a message to the greatest detective she knows.

After receiving a message from Wonder Woman, Batman races to help his friend. He cuts a sharp U-turn across the Metropolis Freeway and steps hard on the Batmobile accelerator. Returning home to Gotham will have to wait.

He scans the city to find Superman and measures his brain waves. They don't match his normal brain signature. Batman quickly pulls up everything he knows about Darkseid as his vehicle roars toward downtown.

DARKSEID

REAL NAME: UXAS

OCCUPATION: TYRANT

STATUS: VILLAIN

HEIGHT: 8FT 9IN

WEIGHT: 1,815 LBS

EYES: RED

HAIR: NONE

BASE: APOKOLIPS

ABILITIES: IMMENSE STRENGTH, NEAR INVULNERABILITY, OMEGA BEAM BLASTS, TRAVELS THROUGH TIME AND SPACE WITH USE OF MOTHER BOX DEVICE.

Wonder Woman is managing to keep people safe, but she is scrambling. She doesn't want to fight her friend. She clears the passengers off a bus before Superman grabs it, hurling the bus at the Daily Planet building. CRASH!

The crash jolts the building, making Jimmy Olsen drop his camera. Lois scoops it up and hands it right back. "Just keep snapping," she says.

Ten seconds later, the Batmobile screeches to a stop beside Wonder Woman. "What took you so long?" she says.

Batman grunts in response. "Get your Lasso of Truth on him," he says. "He'll be vulnerable to the magic."

Wonder Woman shakes her head. "I've tried. He's too quick and there are too many people to save."

Wonder Woman and Batman try to grab their brainwashed friend, but he flies out of their grasp and blows them flat to the ground. Trees fall down around them.

Batman runs back toward Superman, but this time Darkseid pounds the ground between them. The shock waves send Batman flying back. "Sit, Dark Knight," says Darkseid. "Watch the hero destroy his city."

Superman rips the giant metal globe off the top of the Daily Planet building. He lifts it and slowly lowers himself, ready to throw it right through the steel-and-glass facade. Darkseid nods in approval.

Batman leaps into the air, assisted by Wonder Woman. At the peak of his leap, he throws Wonder Woman's magic lasso, pinning Superman's arms to his side. The massive globe tumbles toward the ground. People shriek and scatter, but Wonder Woman is there to catch it!

"I must destroy Earth and build a new Apokolips," says Superman. "Life and hope are useless."

"That's not who you are," says Batman. "Let Diana's rope bring you back to yourself. Darkseid is the one who's useless here."

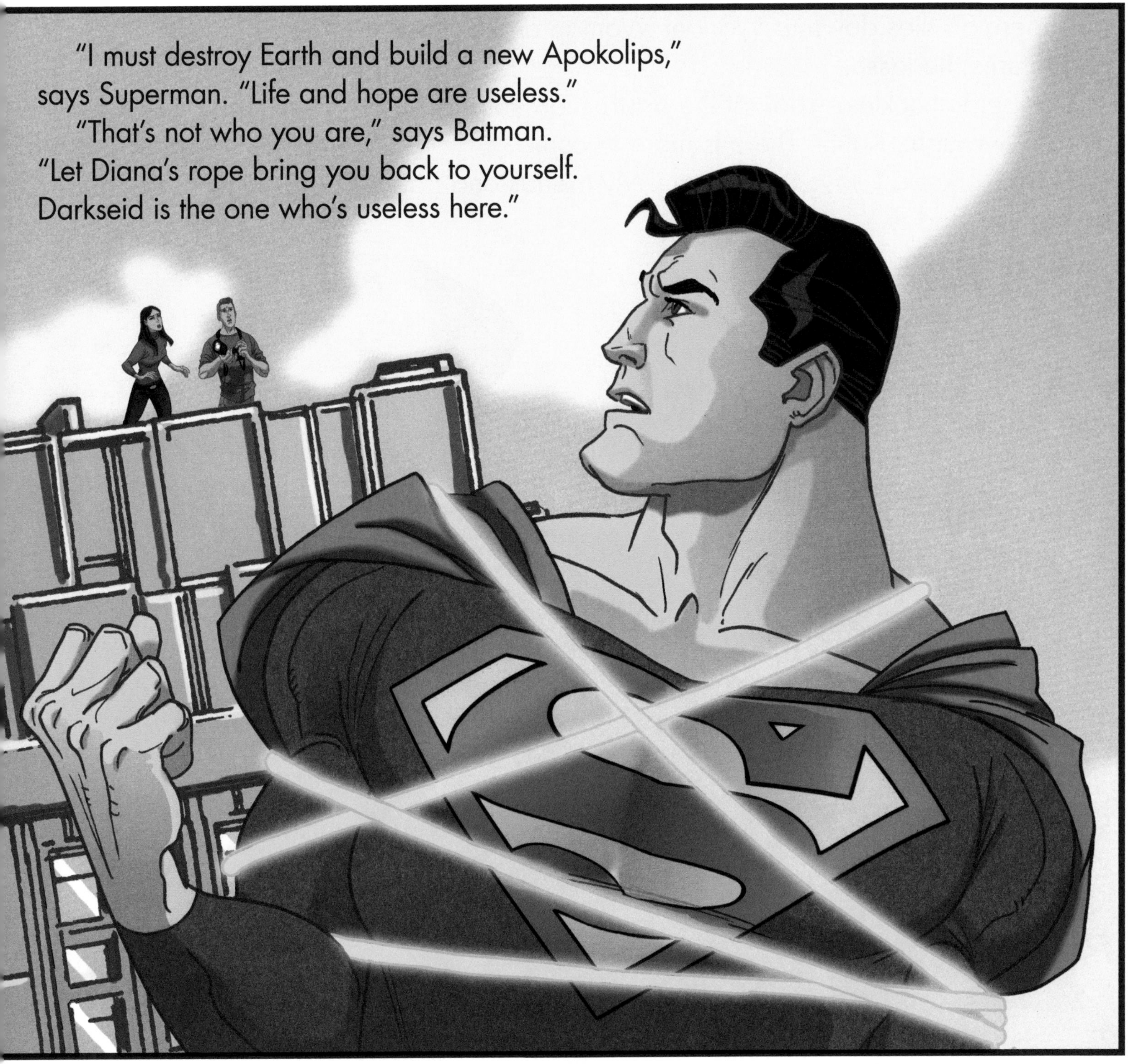

Superman's vision begins to clear. He realizes he is looking right at the Daily Planet roof where Lois and Jimmy are staring back at him. "I'm sorry," he whispers.

Superman flies down to Wonder Woman and Batman and returns the lasso.

Darkseid chuckles. "Look at the destruction you have already wrought, Kal-El. There is more to come."

"No, Darkseid," says Superman. "My friends and I are saving lives today."

Darkseid lets loose his Omega Beams at all three heroes, but Superman acts just as fast. He counters with his own heat vision and the two blasts meet. Superman and Darkseid push closer, each trying to overpower the other.

Batman quickly flips a Batarang at Darkseid, pulling the Mother Box off his suit.

Darkseid is too distracted to notice the device he uses to travel dimensions has been taken.

Batman pulls the box and activates the Boom Tube that will teleport Darkseid across the universe to Apokolips.

"Back to where you came from, Darkseid," mutters Batman.

The heroes help rebuild Metropolis. It will take time to repair everything, but with hope and super heroes, anything is possible.

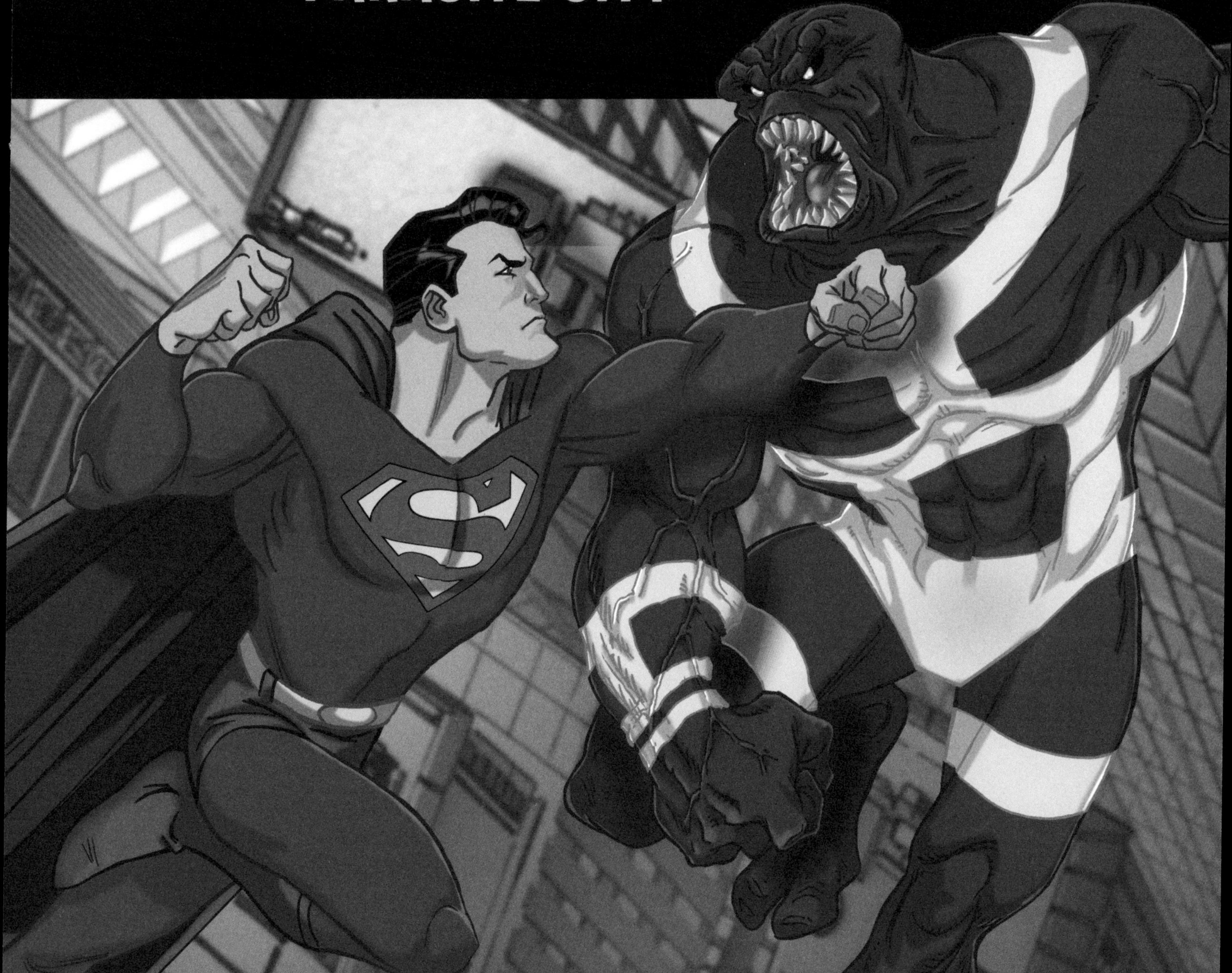

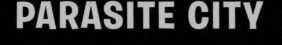

Superman swoops into S.T.A.R. Labs just in time to catch two bad guys struggling with a security alarm.

"Where do you think you're going?" he asks, grabbing the villains and knocking them out cold. "I'll be sure to let the police know where they can find you."

Superman doesn't notice a janitor hiding in the corner of the room. "Look at that," marvels Rudy Jones. "Superman is so strong, he could stop those guys in a second! I wish I could do that."

Superman flies out of the lab. "Wait, Superman!" cries Rudy.

"Come back!" yells the janitor, scrambling for the Man of Steel. He darts toward the window so quickly that he knocks over a waste container. Green goo spills all over him.

"What . . . what's happening to me?" asks Rudy. "I feel so tired and weak . . . and hungry." He crawls toward the bad guys on the ground. "Help me!" he cries, shaking them. A burst of energy runs through Rudy's body the instant he touches the villains. He grows taller and stronger in seconds.

Rudy doubles over in pain as his body changes form and size. "If Superman hadn't flown away, none of this would have happened," he screams. "He is going to pay for this!"

A few hours later, Lois Lane rushes into Clark Kent's office at the Daily Planet building. "Clark! Someone is attacking the mayor! We've got to get to City Hall."

"I'll meet you there, Lois," says Clark. As soon as Lois turns away, Clark changes his clothes and flies out the window—as Superman!

The hero gets to City Hall with super-speed.
He sees a huge, dark creature shaking the mayor.
"Let him go!" says Superman.

"With pleasure," says the creature, dropping the powerless mayor to the ground. "So glad you could make it, Superman."

"Who are you?" asks Superman, getting ready to leap into action.

"Just call me Parasite," says the monster. In a split second, Parasite lunges toward Superman. The hero dashes to the side, but Parasite is too fast. He grabs the Man of Steel. Suddenly, Superman feels very, very tired.

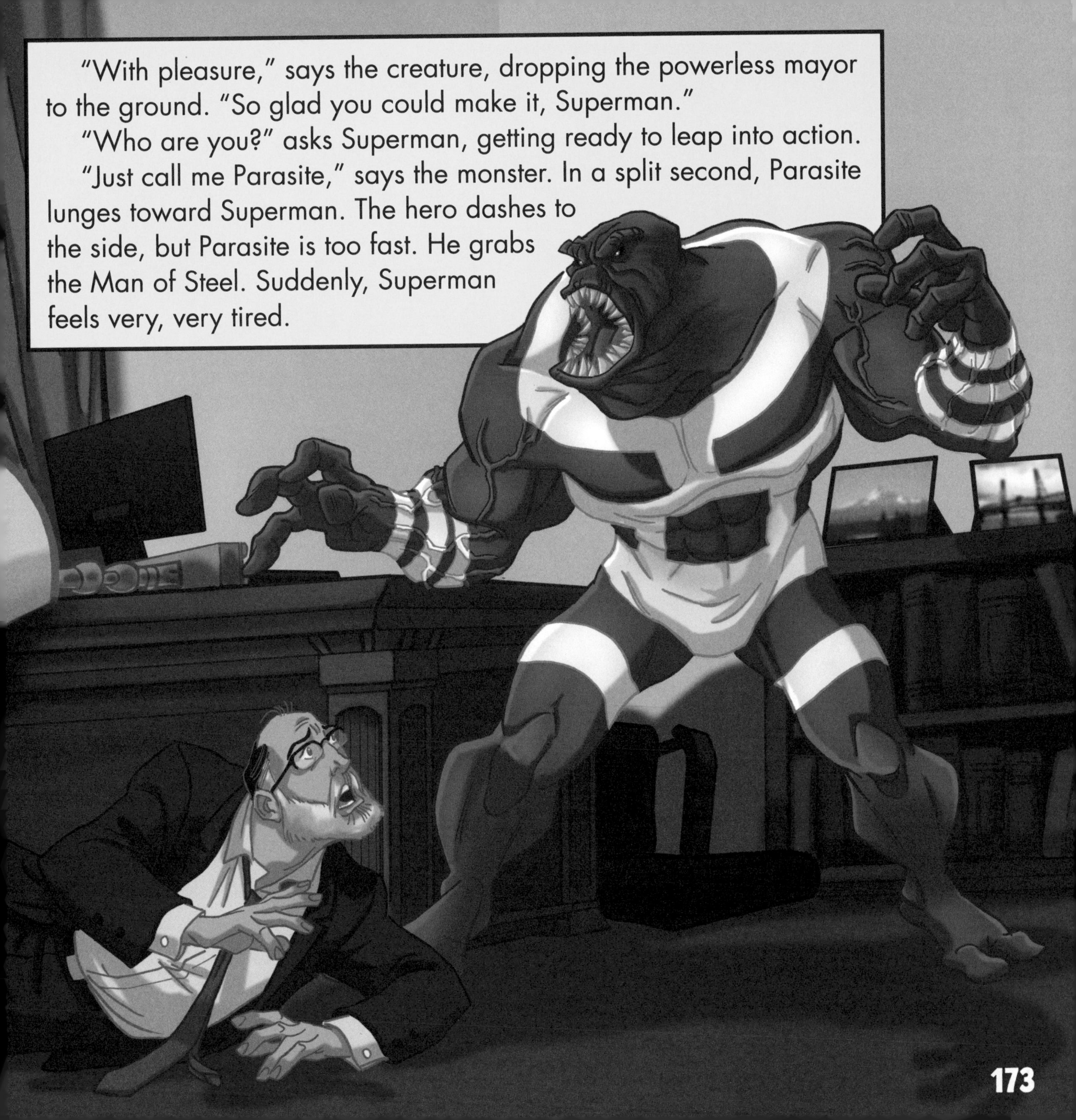

"What's going on here?" Superman says weakly, struggling to get out of Parasite's hold. He tries to use his heat vision and his super-breath—anything to get Parasite to loosen his grip. But all of Superman's powers are gone.

"Thanks for the super-strength, Man of Steel," laughs Parasite coldly. "I'd better keep you around in case I need to recharge. You can be my own private battery!"

Parasite grabs Superman and leaps out of a window. With Superman's powers transferred into his body, the evildoer can fly! He zooms over to S.T.A.R. Labs, locking the hero in the boiler room. "Sit tight, Superman," says Parasite. "I'll be back before you know it."

But the hero recharges faster than Parasite could have imagined. Superman bursts through the boiler room door. "I don't have much time," he says. "I've got to save Metropolis!"

Superman spies a dark shadow in the corner. "A lead suit! This is what the scientists at S.T.A.R. Labs use when they handle dangerous materials." Suddenly, Superman has an idea. Kryptonite can't affect him through lead!

Superman jets downtown just in time to see Parasite tearing down Metropolis's biggest bank. "I hope you've enjoyed your little crime spree, Parasite," yells Superman as he rushes toward his enemy. "It's going to be your last!"

Parasite laughs. "Who's going to stop me?" he cries. "Your silly new suit can't protect you from my strong hold!" Parasite grabs Superman, crushing the hero in his tight grip.

"Feeling sleepy, Superman?" mocks Parasite, expecting his touch to drain Superman of all his strength once again. But the suit's lead lining keeps Superman safe from Parasite's villainous grasp. He breaks free of Parasite and knocks him away, sending the monster reeling!

Parasite is back on his feet in a flash. He slams into Superman, and the two careen through the sky above the streets of Metropolis. "Face it, Superman," Parasite snarls. "I've got your strength. I've got your speed. There's nothing you can do to stop me from crushing you into the pavement!"

"You're right, Parasite," cries Superman. "You stole my biggest strengths. But you got my biggest weakness along with them!" Superman struggles to reach a secret lead-lined pocket inside his suit. With no time left to lose, he pulls out what he is looking for— a piece of kryptonite!

Superman hurls the kryptonite at Parasite. The green rock slams against the villain, shattering into thousands of tiny pieces all over his body. "No!" screams Parasite. "My powers!" He lets go of Superman as he free-falls through the sky.

Superman dives after Parasite, swooping him up and forcing him into the power lines below them. The electricity zaps Parasite of whatever strength he has left.

Soon, the villain is shriveled up like a raisin.
"You'll pay for this, Superman!" squeaks
Parasite weakly.

"I don't think so," says Superman. "You won't be going anywhere for quite
some time. I think I'll hand you over to S.T.A.R. Labs. I'm sure the scientists there
will know just what to do with you."

Back at the Daily Planet building, Lois Lane confronts Clark Kent. "Clark, where were you?" she says. "I can't believe you missed all of the action!"

"Sorry, Lois . . . I wasn't feeling too well," smiles Clark. "I was fighting off a bug."

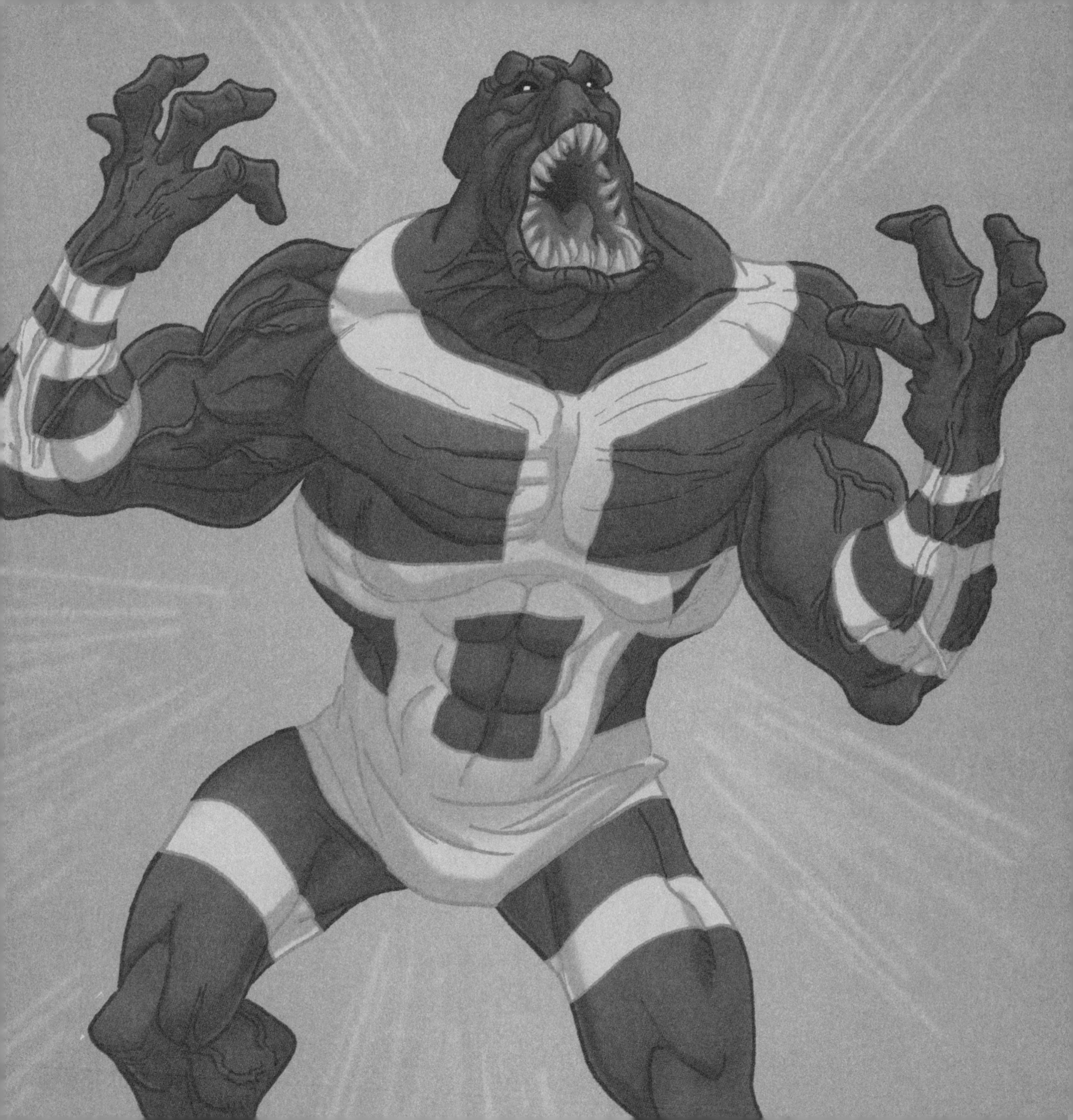

DAILY PLANET

DAILY PLANET

IT'S A BIRD, IT'S A PLANE, IT'S SUPERMAN!

BY LOIS LANE

DC Super Heroes Storybook Collection
Copyright © 2012 DC Comics.
SUPERMAN, BATMAN, WONDER WOMAN, and all related
characters and elements are trademarks of and © DC Comics. (s12)
HARP2599

Batman: Gotham's Villains Unleashed!
By John Sazaklis

Superman and the Mayhem of Metallo
By Sarah Hines Stephens

Batman: Feline Felonies
By John Sazaklis

Superman: The Incredible Shrinking Super Hero!
By Zachary Rau

Batman: Batman and the Toxic Terror
By Jodi Huelin

Batman: Starro and Stripes Forever
By Gina Vivinetto

Superman: Darkseid's Revenge
By Devan Aptekar

Superman: Parasite City
By Lucy Rosen

Printed in the United States of America.
No part of this book may be used or reproduced in any manner
whatsoever without written permission except in the case of brief
quotations embodied in critical articles and reviews. For information
address HarperCollins Children's Books, a division of HarperCollins
Publishers, 10 East 53rd Street, New York, NY 10022.
www.harpercollinschildrens.com

ISBN 978-0-06-212398-5

Book design by Joe Merkel and John Sazaklis

14 15 16 RRDW 10 9

❖
First Edition

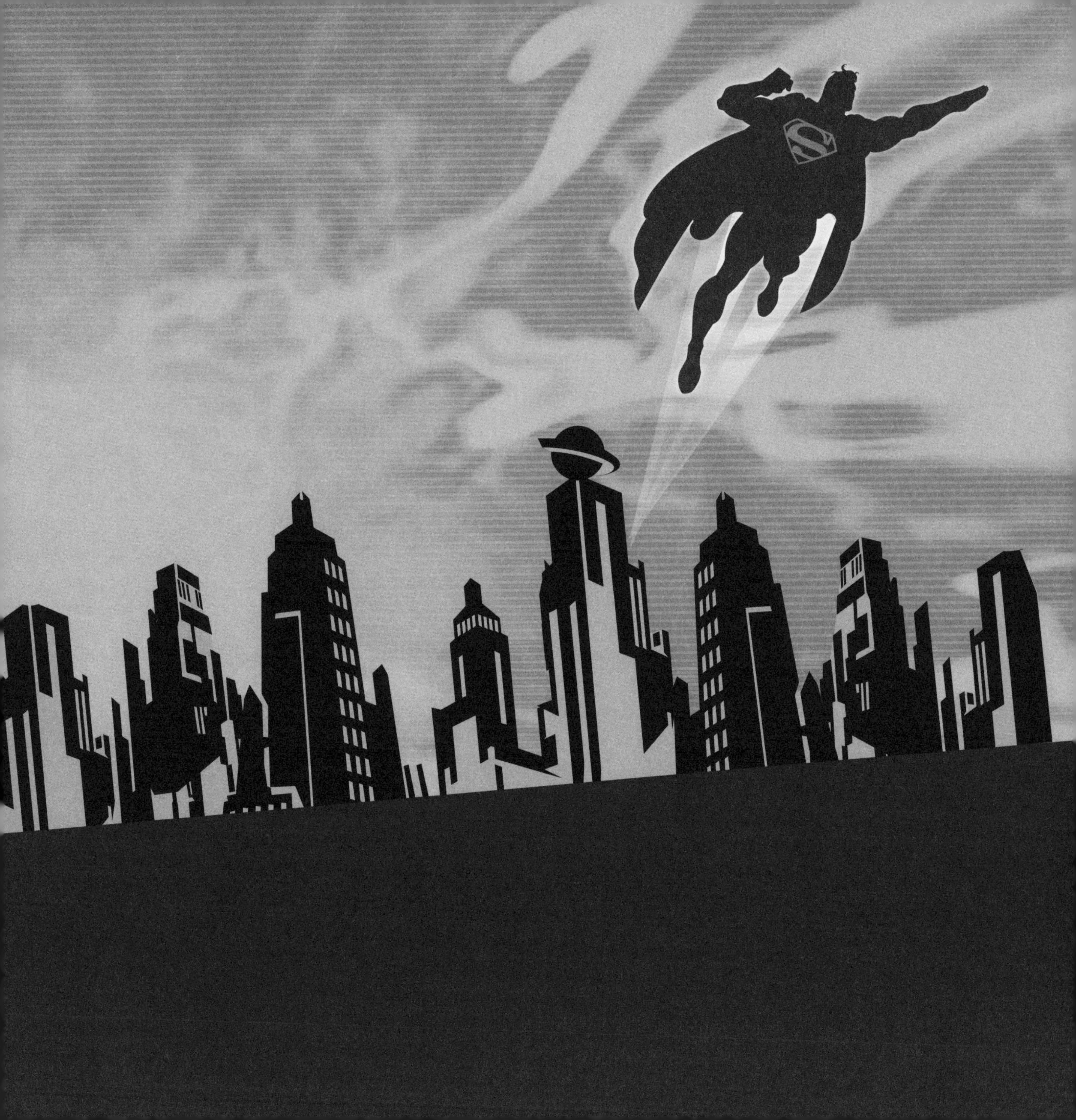

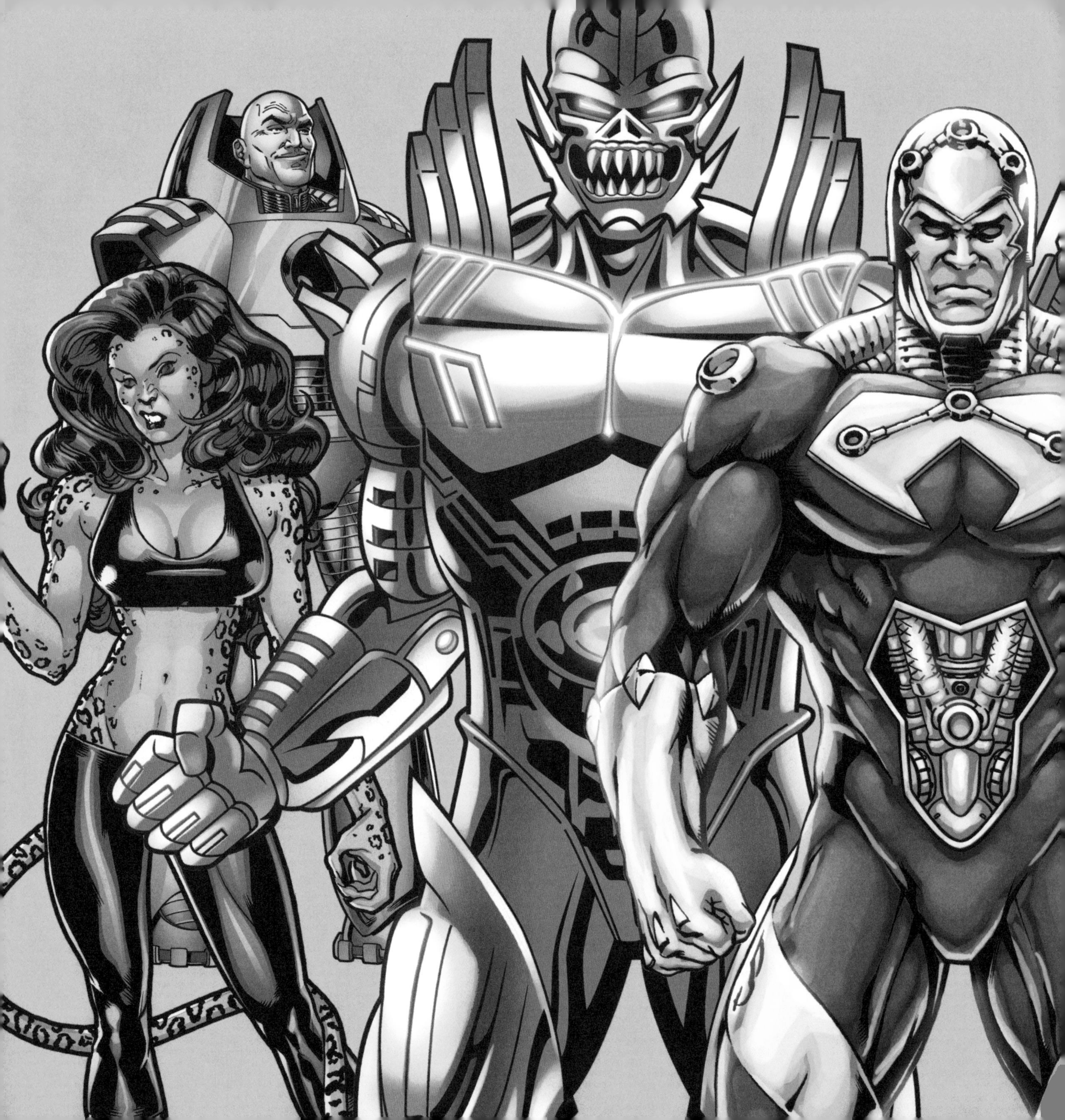

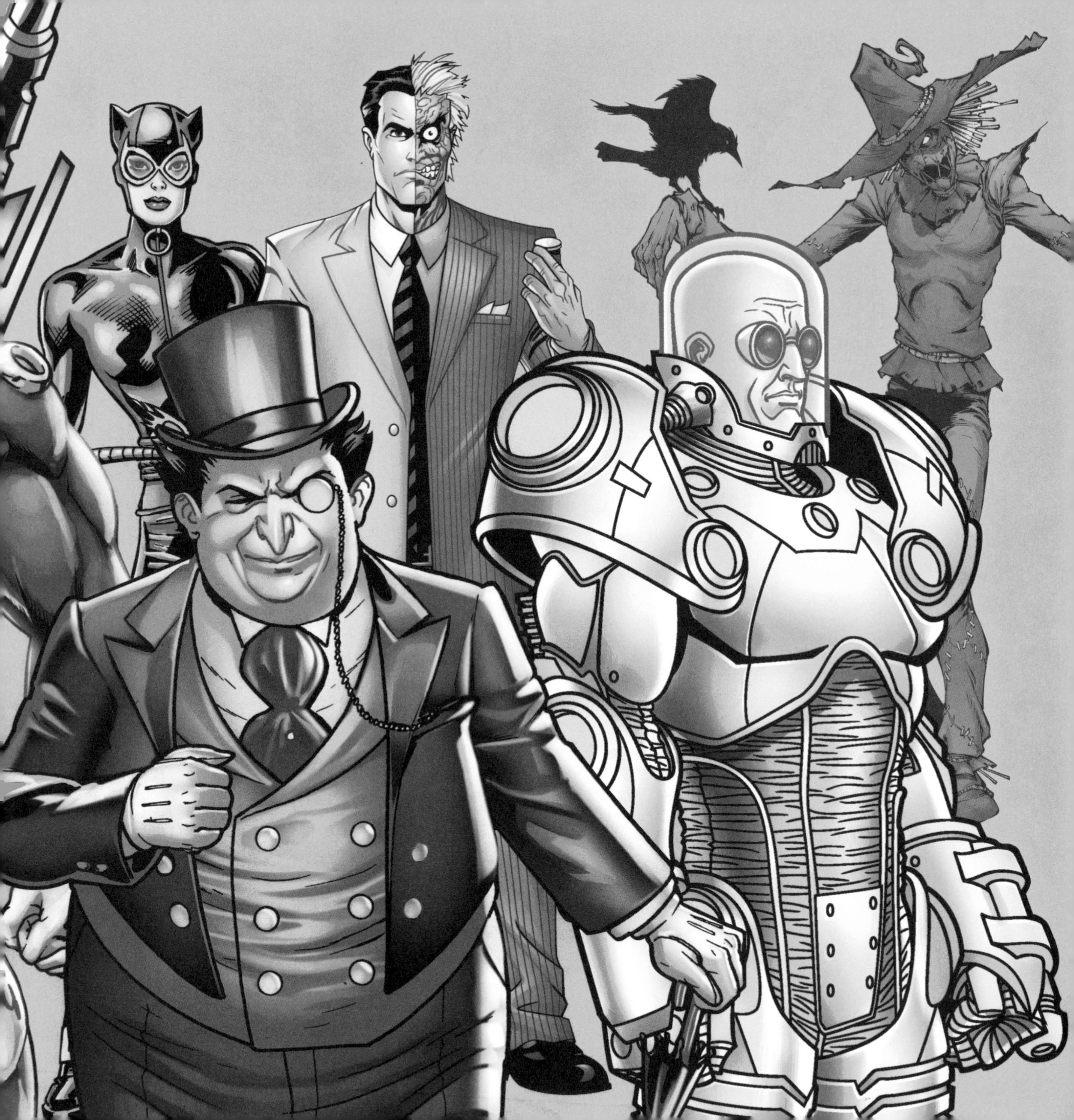

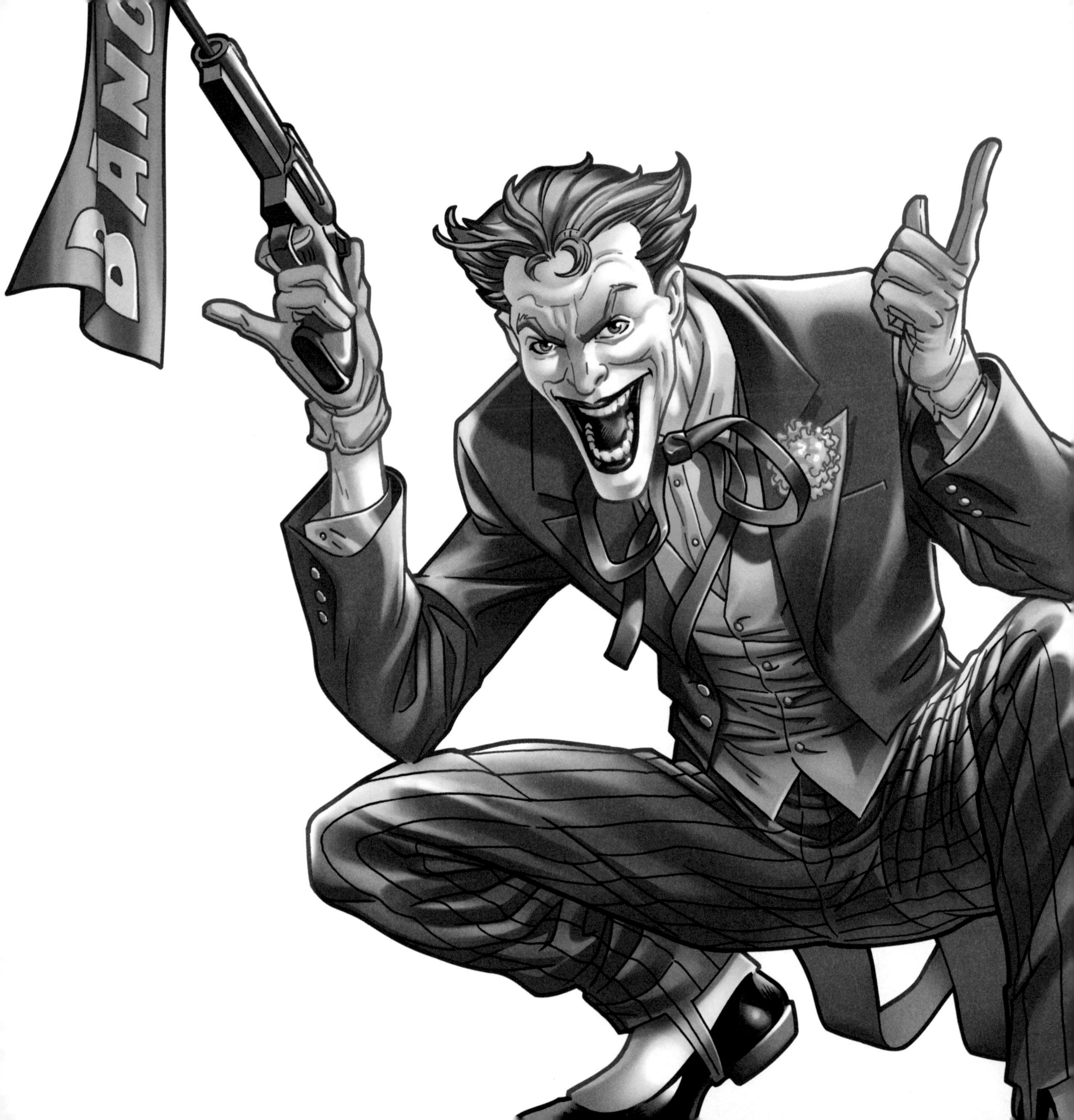
BAN